Alex opened up the email and grimaced—a video.

He clicked on the play button and waited a moment for it to load. Turned the speaker up a touch on his computer and frowned at the poor quality of the picture on his screen. It was black and white. And then he recognized what that small space was—an elevator. And then someone walked into it. And as if he was trapped in it again, free-falling, his stomach dropped.

Hell.

He leaned closer to the screen as she waited in the lift. Her face was clear in the frame, and now so was his as he stood side on, until he turned and faced her. Their mouths were moving, but the security camera recorded images, not sound. Even so, he knew exactly what was being said. He'd replayed that too-brief exchange a million times every sleepless night since.

Alex watched, seeing now what he'd felt so gloriously at the time. His back was to the camera, but you could see her face as he kissed her lips, her jaw, her neck. Her eyes were closed. Her hands caressed his shoulders, his hair. Passionate. Beautiful. And then came the moment her legs parted, wrapped around his waist, and his body reacted now as it had then. Instantly hardening, instantly burning, insisting on getting closer.

And then the lift moved. It had been over far too quickly.

Possibly the only librarian who got told off for talking too much, **NATALIE ANDERSON** decided writing books might be more fun than shelving them—and, boy, is it that! Especially writing romance—it's the realization of a lifetime dream kick-started by many an afternoon spent devouring Grandma's Harlequin romances....

Natalie lives in New Zealand with her husband and four gorgeous-but-exhausting children. Swing by her website, www.natalie-anderson.com, any time—she'd love to hear from you.

Don't miss Natalie Anderson's
sequel to this novel—
on sale February 2011 in
Harlequin Presents Extra.

CAUGHT ON CAMERA WITH THE CEO
NATALIE ANDERSON

~ Unfinished Business ~

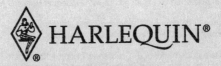

TORONTO • NEW YORK • LONDON
AMSTERDAM • PARIS • SYDNEY • HAMBURG
STOCKHOLM • ATHENS • TOKYO • MILAN • MADRID
PRAGUE • WARSAW • BUDAPEST • AUCKLAND

Recycling programs
for this product may
not exist in your area.

ISBN-13: 978-0-373-52796-0

CAUGHT ON CAMERA WITH THE CEO

First North American Publication 2010.

Copyright © 2010 by Natalie Anderson

CAUGHT ON CAMERA
WITH THE CEO

For the best apple pie and chocolate chip biscuit baker in the world: Aunty Margaret. No one makes 'em like you do. And no one laughs as infectiously as you either. Thank you for all your support.

CHAPTER ONE

'YOU'LL have that for me by three? Fantastic.'

Dani forced her body to freeze at the sound of that voice.

'No problem.'

Dani knew the breathless assistant would have it for him by two at the latest—just as she would if he'd asked her.

Alex Carlisle, CEO of Carlisle Finance Corporation, on his rounds again—gliding through the open-plan area and bewitching his staff so they performed above and beyond. She wondered if he even knew the effect he had on his legions of adoring employees.

And Dani was the latest. Not looking was impossible. Her lashes lifted.

Truthfully she was probably the only one whose work was *suffering* because of him. She found him so distracting she wasn't getting half as much done as she should. Half of her wished he'd go away so her insides wouldn't be so pummelled, but all of her wanted him to stay.

He was so good to look at, she'd been watching him all week. She'd seen how he abandoned his lavish office suite at the top of the building and came to talk with his worker ants—all of whom then frantically tapped faster at keyboards to get the work done for him. Charismatic, confident, Alex Carlisle got everything he wanted, every time. And if the water-cooler gossip she'd got from one of the secretaries was anything to go by, women were a big part of what he wanted—beautiful, high-flying, high-society women. He played a lot, apparently. And all his female employees wished like crazy he'd play with them.

Dani totally understood why they did, but she wasn't going to admit she was floored by him too. So predictable. Anyway she couldn't afford to fixate like this. She checked the time. Only a few minutes and she could go to lunch. She'd never clock-watched before, usually enjoyed her work so the hours flew, but she had a mission to fulfil. Besides, something about this place made her antsy. OK, it was him. She was waiting, always waiting for him to appear. Now he had, she couldn't wait to bust a move, so restless it was as if she had creepy-crawlies infesting every inch of her clothing.

Unable to resist the compelling force of him, she lifted her head and looked again. She was such an idiot. It was as if she'd been tossed into a stormy kind of teen crush—she'd never experienced one in her youth, but it seemed there was a time for everything. She only had to hear his voice for her heart to thunder and the adrenalin to flood her system, so sitting still was no longer possible.

Concentrate, you fool.

The excitement was a waste of energy anyway. The water-cooler woman had also informed her that, while the man might play fast and loose in his own social set, he never ever fooled around at work. Big shame. She watched as he stood talking with her supervisor. He was tall; his tailored trousers seemed to go on forever.

Yeah, Dani, all the way to the floor.

But her self-mockery didn't stop her looking. He'd shed his jacket so he wore just the pale blue shirt, sleeves rolled partially up his arms—the ultimate ad for corporate wear. He turned. Caught her look on the full. And then held it prisoner.

Oh. Wow.

All but his face blurred. The low noise of the office became a distant hum. The sudden silence was nice and her antsy body stopped still, bathed in his gaze. Dani's favourite colour was green. And Alex Carlisle's eyes were very, very green.

He moved, one small step. Was he coming over? To talk to her?

Someone called his name. He turned away, his smile flashing back on. And it was gone—the stillness, the warmth, the quiet. All disappeared the instant she blinked.

Good grief, what was she doing sitting there like a *Muppet*? Unable to move or speak or even breathe? She shook her head and released the air held too long in her straining lungs.

Ridiculous.

But how glad was she that he hadn't come over? Because when he'd looked at her she'd been unable to think of anything. Not a thing. All power had gone from her brain to somewhere else entirely—and was warming her up. She couldn't see how any of them got any work done when he was on the floor.

OK, so it was two minutes 'til lunch. But she'd arrived early, as she always did, and had already promised to work late tonight, so she needn't feel guilty about stepping out now. Because she desperately needed to get outside and gasp in some fresh air.

She walked down the length of the floor to the lift, keeping well to the side of the room. She was short enough not to be noticed and she was only the temp, after all. She moved fast. Usually she took the stairs but he was near the stairs and, as much as she was drawn to him, her instinct told her equally loudly to stay well away. And this instinct was just strong enough to beat the one that made her avoid small, confined spaces. She could do it. Sure she could.

But when she got to the lift and pressed the button, her nerves sharpened. She counted to ten as she waited, trying to slow her breathing to match it with her mental chanting. It was only a lift. People went up and down them millions of times a day without accident. People didn't get trapped in them.

Trapped. Her scalp prickled as if she were under one of those huge cover-your-whole-head driers at the hairdresser— and it was on too hot and she couldn't get it off. She didn't want to be trapped.

She redirected her thoughts. Forced the fear to the back and focused on a plan. If she ate on the run, she'd have time to go to the public library and be able to check the message boards on the Internet. The search was all that mattered.

The lift chimed and she made herself move into it, closing her eyes as the doors slid together. It would be over in a whirl. Such fears were childish.

But there was a noise. She opened her eyes again in time to see the doors sliding back again. An arm was stretching out between them—making them automatically reopen. And stay open.

'I'll be back shortly.' The arm held firm. 'Email the guest list through to Lorenzo, as well, will you? And make sure the catering staff have the right number of vegetarians this time. We don't want to upset anyone again. Oh, and can you make sure Cara gets the message about Saturday?'

Jeez, the lift could have been down and back up again in that time—well, almost. At last, the rest of him stepped in.

He smiled at her. 'Sorry about that.'

Was he really? Or was that just his polite upbringing

talking, hiding the real ramifications of his childhood—that he had the right to make others wait, that his time was more important than hers? Dani only had an hour—unpaid and all—and she had to make the most of it. But that thought and every other disappeared as the doors finally slid shut.

Dani stepped right back, standing stiffly against the far wall of the lift. Would the fear never leave her?

He leant his back against the side wall so he was at right angles to her. Not even covertly looking at her. No, his gaze was open, intense and relentless.

She kept her eyes fixed on the doors, trying to stop the sensation that they were closing in on her. At least the lifts in this building were science-fiction fast—once they were allowed to get started. But the sense of airlessness closed in too.

He pressed the button again and finally it began its swift descent.

Dani gritted her teeth, sweat sliding down her back.

'Are you OK?'

Dani couldn't answer. Too busy holding her breath. Five, four, three…

There was a groaning sound—a metallic moan that, although slow, was definitely getting louder. Dani's muscles flexed. The lift stopped, dropped another foot and then stopped again. Dani's stomach just kept on falling.

She looked at the lights—no floor indicated. The doors half opened and she had a glimpse of metal and concrete. Between floors. She was damn glad when the doors closed again.

There was a second of complete silence.

'I'm sure it won't be long.'

'I'm not worried,' she lied, flicking a glance his way and looking straight back at the doors again when she registered he had a smile on. His smiles weren't good for her blood pressure. Nor was being stuck in a very small space. Adrenalin rippled through her muscles but the nausea rose faster. She inhaled through her nose, aware of every inch of her body. Surely those few years of physical training would stand her in good stead. She could overcome fear. She could breathe.

He'd lifted away from the wall. 'No, really, it won't be long.'

Sure. No matter how stiff she tried to stay, her limbs insisted on shaking. Her heart was shaking too, the beats falling over themselves, and she couldn't breathe fast enough. She couldn't get any oxygen in.

'We never have trouble with these lifts.'

Oh, yeah? Well, they were now. 'You probably confused it by making it wait so long with its doors open,' she said. The spark of anger pushed the bile back down.

'It's a machine. Machines don't get confused. Only people do that.'

She was confused now—her body wanting to run, her brain wanting to shut down altogether, her stomach wanting to hurl its contents.

'You're new here,' he said. 'I've seen you in the office.'

Distraction. Excellent. 'Yes,' she said, barely controlling the wobble in her voice. And after another stumbling beat she looked from the doors to him.

His eyes were very wide and very green and filled with a painfully gentle concern. He took a step towards her. 'My name is—'

'I know who you are,' she cut him off. She couldn't think enough for conversation.

'You do?' His eyes narrowed and his smile twisted, bitterness thinning his sensual lips. 'Then you're one up on me.' He took the last step closing the gap between them. 'I have no idea who I am.'

The bitterness surprised her, blasted the smothering fog from her head. She looked closer at him. 'You're Alex. And you're stuck in a l-lift.'

She glanced at the walls; they were nearing her again. The fear crept back up. She gulped in air. Were they running out of oxygen already? And had she just whimpered?

'There's no need to be afraid.'

Wasn't there? Didn't she know exactly how frightening it was to be stuck in a small place for too long?

'Hey.' He put his hands on her shoulders. 'It's going to be fine.'

At his touch she looked back into his face. Green eyes gazed at her, deepened by the dark lashes that framed them. Everything else in the world receded again. Yes, she'd look at him, focus on him, forget everything…but green eyes. The colour swirled, the black centre spread. His gaze flickered, dropped to her mouth. Made her realise it was dry. She touched her tongue to the corner of it and then she found she was looking at his. It was extraordinarily fine, with lips that were currently curved up in a smile.

'You OK?'

She couldn't take her eyes off him. She couldn't answer.

'Sweetheart?'

Funny how just one word, said in just the right way, could change everything.

She gazed at him, feeling that restlessness inside roar, and her chin lifted.

His hands moved, dropping to circle round her waist.

'It's going to be just fine,' he said. And then slowly, so slowly, giving her all the time to turn away, he lowered his head.

But she didn't turn.

His lips were warm, firm but not forceful, not invasive, just gentle. He lifted his head a millimetre and his green eyes searched hers. 'See?'

Still she said nothing, but the smallest of sighs escaped as she lifted her chin back up to him.

Those strong hands at her waist then lifted her right off her feet. Automatically she put out her own hands—not to punch, but to steady. Her fingers connected with cotton and curled around the hard muscles. The heat of him burned through the shirt. She spread her fingers wider—wow, he was broad. All she could hear was her breathing—too short, too fast.

Their gazes remained locked all the while he lifted her, sliding her up against the back wall of the lift until her eyes were almost level with his. Her heart thundered while her toes stretched down, vainly searching for something solid—like the floor.

This time when he kissed her he stayed, his lips moving over hers slowly teasing. Oh. Her eyes closed as again and again his mouth caressed hers, making her brain go so mushy. And then Dani had to move: softening, opening, relaxing yet seeking at the same time—*more*. And he gave it, his tongue sweeping into her mouth and curling with hers. It was like feeling all her favourite things at once—the heat of a summer's day, the freshness of sea breeze and the sensation of diving into the deepest warm water. Only it was better. It was all-in-one. And it was real.

Her hands slid over his arms, her fingertips exploring his strength and heat, the breadth of his back. She lifted a hand, ran it through his hair. Short, dark, gorgeously thick. She moved, resting her palm on the back of his neck—so warm. Both hands lifted to hold his face close and the kisses changed again—deeper, more hungry, *fevered*. Now every inch of her wanted every inch of him hard up against her. She wanted to feel his body above her, beneath her—all around. But she couldn't tear her mouth from his. She didn't care about the tightness of his hands bruising her waist. She just didn't want the soaring feeling to end. It was as if a veil had been lifted to reveal a bottomless need she hadn't known she had. To be close.

And his need, too, seemed as strong. His kisses on her face and neck were fast, passionate, until their lips connected again and they could plumb the depths of each other in a long, long carnal kiss.

He pulled her away from the wall, close against his body. One hand quickly moving beneath her bottom to take her weight so she didn't fall from his hold. She responded automatically, hooking her legs around his waist. Gasping at how good it felt to have his body between hers. He was big, strong and fantastically hard. Basic instinct screamed at her now. Bursting with need for bare skin, she pressed her mouth harder against his, her fingers fighting with his shirt.

But then she felt him stagger. He pushed her, lifting her away and down until her feet hit the ground. But then the ground itself bumped up and down.

Oh, no, that was right. They were in a lift. Dani tore her gaze away from him. Looked beyond to the lights, to the door. The lift had finally moved again, descended. And now those doors were opening.

'I—'

He didn't get a chance to say whatever it was he was going to say. There were people—bankers, a couple of technicians. All chorusing his name.

'Alex!'

Dani knew when to make the most of an opportunity. Her legs might be short but she could move them quickly. And, breathless though she was, she had a huge hit of adrenalin to see her through. Energy was an inferno inside her roaring for release. Her high heels clipped on the polished floor. As she exited through the big glass door she glanced back. He was still caught talking to the group. Frowning this time, no smile. And he glanced up frequently, tracking her, she knew. Sparkling light tumbled from his eyes towards her. She walked faster. Pulled her mobile from the bag that miraculously was still slung over her shoulder. She'd phone the agency. Find another job. Snogging the boss was so not allowed. But it wasn't her flouting of that convention that made her move so fast. It was the fear of that bottomless need he'd uncovered. And the truth that she was desperately trying to ignore: it hadn't been a *snog*, it had been heaven.

Alex lifted the cup and sipped—yick. He might be sprawled in a big chair in the first-class club but the coffee was still thin, airport dross. He glanced at his laptop on the table beside him. The screen saver had been dancing for a good twenty minutes now—hiding the report he should have finished already. But focus had been impossible when distraction had such curves. He should be working. And if he wasn't working he should be worrying about Patrick's bombshell last week and the horrendous ramifications of those test results. He should be dealing with it.

Instead he was indulging in a wicked fantasy and debating how he was going to turn it into reality. There simply had to be more—wrong though it was. But those minutes in the elevator with that petite temp had been magic, and not anywhere near enough. Since when did he start kissing random women in elevators? Especially an employee? Just because she'd been nervous?

Well, it had seemed like a good way of distracting her at

the time. And himself. But that irresistible distraction had turned searingly, mind-blowingly incredible—how was he going to ensure he got more?

His mobile chimed. Lorenzo. Alex answered promptly. 'Hey.'

'Where are you?'

'Sydney Airport.'

'Man, you're hardly ever home these days.'

Alex sighed. 'I know. Just waiting for the flight back.'

He'd arranged this business trip after Patrick had called out of the blue. After years of only occasional correspondence, he'd rung to tell him the 'truth'—thirty years too late. At first Alex hadn't believed him, had insisted on the tests. It had only taken twenty-four hours. After seeing it in black-and-white he'd had to get away. He could have done the deal with conference calls, but he'd used it to avoid everyone for a few days. But now the job was done and he was aching to get back to Auckland. He had unfinished business to tend to and it wasn't the paternity nightmare.

'There's something you've got to see.'

Alex sat up, registering the thread of tension in Lorenzo's usually dry-humoured tones. Instinctively he pressed the phone closer to his ear to catch the nuances better. 'What is it?'

'You need to see it. I've sent you the link. You should have it now.'

He reached out and tapped a couple of buttons on the laptop, Lorenzo's email opened up and he grimaced—a YouTube video. 'Its not some stupid joke, is it?'

'I don't think so.' For once Lorenzo actually sounded unsure.

'Not porn?' He might be the boss, but the 'inappropriate use of office computers' clause applied to him too.

'Uh, well, I don't think so.' There was a laugh now. 'Just watch it, Alex.'

He read the title 'Get Stuck, Get Snogged—is this the hottest kiss ever?' and groaned. 'Lorenzo, it is porn.'

'Just watch it.'

He clicked on the play button and waited a moment for it to load. Turned the speaker up a touch on his computer and frowned at the poor quality of the picture on screen. It was black-and-white. And then he recognised what that small space was—an elevator. And then someone walked into it. And as if he was were trapped in it again, freefalling, his stomach dropped.

Hell.

That awful music hadn't been playing. Muzak didn't play in the lifts at all; no point when they whisked you up and down the many stories so fast—or at least they did if they weren't faulty and hadn't stopped between floors.

When that had happened, five days ago, it had been silent, save her breathing, which—despite her efforts to control it—had spiked. So whoever had lifted this footage had added a cheesy soundtrack—rich, melted chocolate, 'in the mood' kind of music. It didn't fit.

He leant closer to the screen as she waited in the lift. Her face was clear in the frame, and now so was his as he stood side on, until he turned and faced her. She didn't look nervous in this, but up close she'd been shaking like a leaf. Their mouths were moving, but the security camera recorded images, not sound. Even so, he knew exactly what was being said. He'd replayed that too-brief exchange a million times every sleepless night since.

And he knew her face too well. He'd been prowling the floor more than usual just to get a glimpse after spotting her in the open-plan office on Monday. Her glossy black bob with the too-long fringe had caught his eye, and then her oh-so-professional man-style shirts hinted at the most luscious curves.

The last thing he should be doing was chasing skirt—walking through the office a zillion times a day on the lamest of excuses. But while waiting on those blood results he'd been only too happy to be distracted. For five minutes he hadn't wanted to think at all. So he hadn't. And the moment he'd touched her, all remaining rational thought had fled. Her shape was more wicked than he'd suspected—slim, soft, devastatingly curvaceous. It hadn't taken much effort at all to lift her against the back wall of the elevator, raising her high enough so her eyes were almost level with his. Beautiful big brown eyes burnished with a caramel gold—and filled with a challenge he'd been utterly unable to resist. He'd been thinking about what she'd feel like in his arms—dreaming of her curves spilling into his hands. Damn it, he was still dreaming of that.

Alex blinked, came out of the haze and watched, seeing now what he'd felt so gloriously at the time. His back was to the camera but you could see her face as he kissed her lips, her jaw, her neck. Her eyes were closed, her hands caressed his shoulders, his hair. Passionate. Beautiful. And then came the moment, her legs parted, wrapped around his waist and his body reacted now as it had then. Instantly hardening, instantly burning, insisting on getting closer.

And then the bloody lift moved. It had been over far too quickly.

'You're watching it again, aren't you?'

Alex flinched. Hell, he'd forgotten Lorenzo was still on the phone. He'd forgotten he was sitting in an airport lounge. Fortunately it was a midweek red-eye flight and the other patrons were too busy slurping the rotten coffee to pay any attention to him.

'It looks pretty good,' Lorenzo added blandly. 'You're getting some star ratings.'

Alex scrolled down, read the first few comments and felt his face fire up like some mortified teen caught making out with his first girlfriend—by his grandma.

'Who is she?' Lorenzo might sound indifferent, but Alex knew his friend was as agog as he got.

'I don't know.'

'What do you mean you don't know?'

'She's a temp. Started last week. I don't know her name.'

Lorenzo's chuckle didn't help. 'Well, you better find out—this thing is doing the rounds of every inbox in the office.'

'You're kidding.'

'Wish I was, but I've been sent it three times already this morning—and once from a colleague in Hong Kong.'

Anger surged into Alex's veins. He didn't need this and she didn't deserve it. It had been a whim—a crazy, lusty whim and one right on the edge of his code. Alex Carlisle never seduced temps or coworkers—too messy. Especially given he was the boss. But the irresistible force of her had felled him. And was still affecting him—wasn't that why he was sitting here now doing nothing? Despite having been up for hours he hadn't achieved a thing because he was too busy plotting how he could get close to her again as soon as he got back to Auckland. How did he do it without breaking his own rules?

'What would your old man say?' Lorenzo laughed again. 'Screwing around in the office, Alex, bad you.'

Alex iced over and pressed pause on the playback. He hadn't told Lorenzo what he'd found out. It was proved—the chance of the DNA results being wrong were so tiny no lawyer in the land would dare argue it. Samuel Carlisle wasn't Alex's father. Instead it was his best friend who'd supplied the necessary chromosomes. The friend who'd been on the periphery of Alex's childhood—the honorary uncle, the godfather figure—

hell, he'd even been the one to offer advice when Alex had doubted whether he'd wanted to go into the family business.

'You're a Carlisle—it's in your blood.'

Patrick had lied so easily.

Alex had found out only a few years after that that Samuel couldn't be his biological father. When illness had struck, Alex had offered his body, his blood. But it didn't match Samuel's—*at all*. His mother had begged him not to tell, but she'd refused to say who his real father was. She'd taken that secret to the grave with her.

Alex couldn't then ask Samuel—couldn't destroy his last years. But Alex had been burnt through from the inside out by the betrayal. Anger, resentment had festered, his trust severed. And in the quiet dark hours the unanswered question had tormented him.

But now he knew. Patrick had been her lover. Patrick had fathered her child. The pair of them had lied for years to the man she was married to. They'd lied to him, their son.

And Alex would never forgive either of them for it.

He needed time before he could speak of it—even to his best friend. But before he got to that, there was now this situation to be sorted.

He forced out a half-laugh as he looked at the image on screen. Caught out the one time he went base at work. Just the icing on the way the last week had gone.

'I'm flying back shortly. Meet me at my place this afternoon.' He hung up before Lorenzo could say more. Stared at the way her hands threaded through his hair and her legs clamped round his waist.

The anger simmering beneath his skin spiked through. He wished he could storm into Security, find the culprits and fire them on the spot. Every single one of them. But going on the hunt would only inflame the situation. He'd have to make do with a memo reminding them of the 'Use of Internet' policy. He couldn't get rid of them—at least, not yet.

Damn.

The other person he couldn't sack was her—straight to litigation that would be. But it was going to be pretty messy with everyone in the office watching this little number. How was he going to protect her?

He didn't even know her name.

CHAPTER TWO

DANI wondered what it was she'd done wrong. She'd been temping here for over a week and until today they'd all been polite and friendly. All except Mr Alex Carlisle, that was. But she wasn't thinking about him. Definitely not fixated on what had to have been the craziest few minutes of her life. She'd forget it. He obviously had, because she hadn't seen him since—he'd disappeared from the floor, hadn't been down loitering by the managers' desks at all since The Lift. She refused to acknowledge the sting she felt over that. And she hadn't been able to swap to a placement with another company; there were no other placements—none that lasted as long and paid the same kind of money. So, embarrassed or not, she was here to stay.

But the looks she was getting from everyone else today. The number of people that had filed past her desk…and they'd all been rubbernecking. There was no way they could know what had happened. He wouldn't have told anyone, would he?

Maybe she had half her breakfast on her face. She ducked behind her computer screen and used a tissue. Surely they didn't know. How could they? They'd been alone. It hadn't been long—not nearly long enough for her starved hormones—only a few minutes. They'd been a metre apart when those lift doors opened because he'd been aware enough to move. She hadn't. So, given that he'd moved, he hadn't wanted them to be caught. Therefore, Dani reasoned, they couldn't know and she was just feeling paranoid. Besides, it was days ago now. And she. Had. Forgotten. It.

But there was an unnatural awareness about the place. She could feel them all watching her. And she couldn't help but think of him again. She'd been told he had a way with women, but she hadn't realised he had more pulling power than the sun.

She couldn't put all the responsibility on him, though, could she—hadn't she deliberately lifted her chin at him? Hadn't she deliberately looked him over as he had her? Hadn't she widened her stance—preparing for battle but also preparing for contact?

She had. And she hadn't exactly given him a cool, back-off response. She'd enjoyed every second of it, far more than she'd thought it was possible to enjoy a kiss. And that was terrifying. To want like that made you weak.

The office stirred, as if an invisible wave were working its way through. She glanced over her screen. Not invisible. This was a tidal wave and she was in its path—for that was the HR dragon, wasn't it, heading straight for her?

'Danielle? Could you come with me, please?'

For some reason a power-that-be like her could make Dani feel guilty just by the way she said her name. But Dani hadn't done anything wrong. OK, she hadn't been quite at her usual output level, but she hadn't been bad. Something was definitely up. She was aware of the sudden stillness in the office—no one was talking, no one was moving. They were all, she realised, watching her. She lifted her head that little bit higher—*don't show weakness*.

'Shall we take the lift?' The dragon seemed to have a gleam in her eyes.

No way could she know about the lift. Could she? 'I'd prefer the stairs,' Dani answered quietly.

That was definitely a smirk. Quickly covered, but it had flashed in her eyes and on the edges of her mouth. Then there was nothing—just chilly silence all the way up the stairs to the executive level, even heavier silence in the corridor, only when the door closed behind her as she entered the woman's office was there the slightest noise. She wasn't invited to sit down. The woman just turned and spoke.

'I'm sorry but your recruitment agency has been in touch. Apparently there is a problem with your file.'

'A problem?' What kind of problem? Dani's blood ran cold. Surely it wasn't about her father. She'd passed bank security clearances in Australia despite his record. They'd investigated and known it was nothing to do with her—that she'd been a victim as much as the others he'd ripped off. But maybe in New Zealand they had different rules?

'I'm not entirely sure—you'll need to talk to your agent about that. However—' the woman was robot-like '—it means we're unable to have you working here any longer.'

'*What?*' She couldn't lose this job. She just couldn't. She was down to her last dollars. Literally—her last fifty or so. She'd come over too soon, hadn't saved enough, but she'd been so lonely and so desperate to find him. She'd waited long enough—so had he.

'The agency has the money for the days you've already worked this week. If you go and see them, you'll be able to collect it.' Her tone was utterly dismissive. Final.

'I'm to go now?' Dani gaped.

'Yes. Gather your belongings and leave immediately.'

Dani clocked the woman's impassivity. Wow—how could she ruin someone's life and look so uncaring?

She turned and left the room, tightening every muscle hard to stop the trembling from being visible. She walked back down the empty corridor to the stairs. This just couldn't be happening. It just couldn't. Her paperwork was totally fine; she was sure of it. When she'd registered with the agency they'd been pleased with her qualifications and experience. So, there was no problem—unless someone had taken a dislike to her?

Someone *important*?

She stopped. Swallowed. Turned and walked back—all the way to the corner office and to the fiftysomething woman sitting guard-like outside the sanctum.

'Is Mr Carlisle in?' Despite her determination it was only a whisper that sounded.

'He's overseas,' his PA answered crisply.

How convenient. Dani's suspicions grew, edging out the anxiety. 'When is he back?'

The PA lifted her head and looked at her. Behind the old-school librarian glasses she seemed to be reading her for a long moment before her lashes dropped. 'I believe he's due back here early this afternoon.'

And she'd be gone by then. Doubly convenient.

No way was this a coincidence. He didn't want to be embarrassed at work—was that it? Had she been so all over him he was trying to get rid an awkward situation before it got even more complicated? What was he afraid of—that she'd go psycho stalker on him?

She turned on the spot and marched back down the stairs to her floor. She'd go straight to the agency and clear it up. She needed the money more than he needed a clear-conscience office.

'Hi, Danielle.' One of the young bankers gave her a leery grin when she walked past him. He hadn't spoken to her before. She caught the grins then swapping between him and some of the others. It had probably been a bet. She knew about boys and their bets—ones made at her expense.

She didn't have the time or capacity to deal him even a cool look. Too busy trying to stomach the sick feeling. She'd been in the country less than a fortnight, was on the bones of her butt in terms of funds and now she'd just lost her job. And she needed to know *why*.

It only took two minutes to get her jacket from the back of her seat and the bag she'd tucked under the table. She logged off her computer.

She turned. The office was so quiet she would have heard her now ex-colleagues blinking—if they weren't all staring totally bug eyed at her. Wow, the ones down the far end had actually risen out of their chairs to get a better look. What on earth was going on?

She tossed her head, determined to hide the freak-out thudding of her heart. So what if her cheeks were purple with embarrassment—she could still walk, right? OK, it was a run/walk to the door and after that she basically threw herself down the stairs, letting the adrenalin fly to her feet.

The recruitment agency was only a ten-minute walk away. Dani did it in seven. Red cheeked, breathless, trying to suck up the desperation pouring out of her.

Then she had to wait ten extra-long, make-you-sweat minutes.

'What's the problem with my file?' Dani asked as soon as she was shown in.

'There are a couple of issues.' The agent wouldn't look her in the eye. 'One is misconduct.'

Misconduct? Dani frowned, that she hadn't expected. 'What kind of misconduct?'

The woman smiled then—it wasn't a kind smile. 'Have you seen this?' She angled her computer screen so Dani could see it.

Dani gripped her bag, pushing it hard on her lap as she waited for the clip to start playing. Why was she being shown a vid on YouTube? What was this all about?

She squinted at the black-and-white grainy images. Oh, no. It couldn't be.

Not *her*.

Not *him*.

OMG—it was! Alex Carlisle and her, Dani Russo, locking lips in that damn lift. Oh, *more* than locking lips. There was neck kissing, and touching and *moving*.

Heat prickled all over her body. From every pore popped a painful drop of blood. How had this happened? This just had to be a joke. Was she in a reality TV show and she didn't know it?

'Where did you get that?' she whispered, knowing she was damned.

'It was emailed to us. I believe it's been circulated around the company already.'

So that explained the staring, then. The embarrassment engulfed her, swamping the spark of anger she'd felt before.

The agent didn't stop the clip playing, just sat blandly waiting. Three and a half minutes of absolute agony. Dani couldn't look away from the screen. Had they been so passionate? Had she really jumped on him like that? Had she been so hungry? And what was that awful music?

Not going to cry. Not going to cry.

She hadn't in years. And she wouldn't, not 'til she was alone.

Finally it ended. Dani couldn't look at the woman.

'But this isn't why we're unable to place you in another position.'

Dani didn't understand. 'Pardon?' Still shocked.

'This was obviously a mistake and an embarrassing one, but we can deal with it with a simple warning.' The agent couldn't be crisper. 'Not on work time, not on work premises. Understand?'

Dani just nodded. Still unable to process what she'd just seen—they'd been filmed? How was that possible?

'The reason we've had to pull you from the job is because we haven't been able to get your school records verified.'

Dani jerked. Her *school* records? How were they relevant? She had banking qualifications that totally surpassed her achievements at school. Plus she had her security clearance from the Australian bank she'd worked at for the last three years—surely that was far more important than verifying her school-leaver's certificate?

'I can call the school,' she said. 'I can get them to fax whatever you need.'

'No, that's fine. We'll keep trying.' The woman smiled sharply. 'But until we do get it, we can't put you into another placement.'

It was then that Dani knew and understood. They weren't trying to contact the school; even if they did there would be some other obstacle that would arise. This was about that video—her fooling with the boss and getting caught. The school-records thing was an excuse. The walls were up. Her anger surged then, pushing back the embarrassment. 'I can go to other agencies?'

'Of course.' The woman smiled. 'But you might encounter the same problem.'

Dani looked at the computer screen again. Yeah, that was the real problem. She could see how many hits the clip had had. Too many just to be the bank staff and this agency—even if they had watched it over and over as she was quite sure some of those sleazy bankers had. No, this one had been doing the rounds; it would be a source of great amusement for anyone in the industries—both finance and recruitment. Alex Carlisle proving his legendary swordsman status with a temp at work.

There was nothing for it but to make a dignified exit. No way could she win this battle here and now. She needed to withdraw and come up with some kind of strategy.

She stood, stuck a small smile on her numb face. 'Thank you for letting me know. Please get in touch when you get my record confirmed. I'd like to get working as soon as I can.'

'Of course.' The agent stood and saw her to the door.

It was a complete fiction. They both knew they were never going to talk to each other again.

'You can collect your wages for the last couple of days from Reception.'

Dani made for the nearest café and ordered the biggest blackest coffee they made. She closed her eyes. The money she had would last less than a week. Her whole aim had been to work while she hunted because she hadn't wanted to wait any longer before trying to find him. But she had to be able to eat—to pay for her accommodation, and to pay for the search. How on earth was she going to find Eli now? How was she going to keep the promise she'd made to her mum?

It had been her final request—she'd given up that precious secret only in her last few days and it was the one last thing Dani *could* do for her. Dani wanted to honour that promise more than she wanted to do anything. And if she found him, it would be like having a part of her mother back.

She called a different agency. Then another. But once she'd told them the kind of work she wanted, then told them her name, the 'our books are full' line got handed to her. Was she going to have to move cities to get another job? She didn't even have the bus fare, and the best finance jobs for her were here. Or they had been. Now she was screwed.

Her anger fired even higher. What about Alex Carlisle? What about his misconduct? Had he been given a 'warning'— she bet there was no way he'd have got the sack. Oh, no— he'd just ensured he had a peaceful work environment again. She wasn't around to embarrass him anymore.

There was one person responsible for this. One person who owed her. One person who was going to pay.

Alex Carlisle was getting the bill.

'Kelly, I need you.' Alex called his PA into his office. 'The temp who was working on the Huntsman project last week—' He broke off. His super-efficient PA had a touch more colour to her cheeks than usual. But her brows lifted as if she were vaguely mystified.

As if.

'Temp?'

'Yes. Short, brunette bob.' Alex winced, hating to have to reveal that he didn't know her name. He watched Kelly's lips purse and sighed, frustrated. 'You've seen the clip, haven't you?' Now he felt his cheeks heating.

Kelly dropped the 'no idea' look and nodded. 'Yes. She no longer works here.'

'How come she's no longer working here? That project is months off completion.' Alex found he couldn't meet Kelly's eyes. Hell, what a mess. He'd never compromised himself at work like this. Socially for sure—he liked to play. But not at work. Kelly had worked for this company for more years than he'd been alive. She'd worked with Samuel, and his father before him. A Carlisle loyalist. There was nothing in the business that she didn't know. Alex remembered her giving him paper as a kid to entertain him while he waited for Samuel and him making darts to shoot at people walking past. The severe look she was giving him now wasn't so different from the one she'd given him then.

'I know,' Kelly said quietly. 'But there's a new temp now.'

Alex looked at her then, hearing the soberness in her voice. He didn't like the censure in her eyes, either. 'I think you'd better send Jo to see me.'

Kelly disappeared and Jo, the head of HR, was knocking at his door in less than a minute. Alex walked over to meet her. 'The temp that we had working on the Huntsman project last week—where is she?'

Jo looked distinctly uncomfortable. 'The temp?'

'Yes,' he growled. 'You know the one I mean.'

'Yes.' Of course she did. 'Her services were no longer required.'

'But there's a new temp out there now.' He'd walked through the floor as soon as he'd got in, run the gauntlet of knowing looks and smiles only to be completely disappointed when it had been some blonde at the desk and not the little brunette who'd been haunting him for days. 'So why did you get rid of the other one? On whose authority? For what reason?' He rapped out the questions, the nasty feeling in his gut growing.

Jo looked even more uncomfortable. 'It was the recruitment agency. They phoned and said they'd made a mistake with her file. They hadn't been able to verify her school qualifications so they pulled her.'

Alex stared at her, anger churning. 'So she's no longer working for the agency?'

'No. I don't believe she is.'

It was his turn to take a deep breath—he had to force his jaw apart to do it. 'They couldn't verify her school qualifications?' Alex shook his head. 'But we had security clearance for her? And proof of her banking exams?'

'Yes.'

So the records meant diddly, then. If she had her banking qualifications, then they didn't need to verify any other records—she couldn't have got the bank ones if she hadn't had the school ones. It was a trumped up excuse to get rid of her.

'So it wouldn't have had anything to do with this?' He strode to his desk and spun his computer screen round so the image he'd paused it on was viewable from her side of the room.

His head of HR went beet red.

Alex leaned back on his desk and folded his arms, hiding the fists. 'Don't tell me you haven't seen it. Everyone in the office has seen it. Haven't they?'

Jo nodded.

'And now you're telling me she's been removed for the most flimsy of reasons.'

'We're covered, Alex. It was the agency who removed her. Her dismissal had nothing to do with this…incident.'

Alex stared at her, unable to believe his ears. Like hell it didn't. She'd done nothing wrong. She shouldn't have lost her job. His fists bunched tighter.

'Does she have another job?' He could only hope she had a better one.

'I don't know.'

'Then you better phone the agency and find out,' he growled—he was not going to be able to rest until he knew. The job market was horrendous at the moment. That meant the temp market was even more vicious.

'Excuse me, Alex.' Kelly came back in, shutting the door

fast behind her and stepping forward. 'I have someone outside insisting on seeing you.'

'Who is it?' Alex asked crossly. 'I don't want interruptions now, Kelly.'

'I know you don't. But this one is different. It's her.'

'Who?'

'That temp.'

Alex froze. 'She's here?'

Kelly nodded.

'Now?' The ripple that ran through his body was pure testosterone. 'You. Out,' he barked at Jo.

She was out of there faster than a condemned prisoner getting a last-minute reprieve. But Alex was the one feeling the edge of desperation. He turned to the woman who knew more about what went on in the building than anyone. 'Kelly, please, what's her name?'

Kelly looked up at him through her half-glasses, her face as impassive and composed as always. When she finally answered, it was with marked deliberation. 'You really ought to know that already.' Then she left.

Alex stared at the door and wondered how on earth he was going to get away with it.

Dani perched on the edge of the chair—the one nearest to the exit. She shouldn't have come. What was she doing back here? Sweating for one thing and she was all shaky inside, as if it wouldn't take much for tears to sting. She couldn't let that happen—getting all emo was one sure way to come off the loser. She blinked and went rigid as the hideous HR dragon appeared from his office. She glanced at Dani but made no acknowledgement as she swept past. That was it—Dani was leaving. What had possessed her to attempt this? Oh, yeah, desperation.

Now the PA was standing in front of her. 'Mr Carlisle will see you now.'

Mr Carlisle. She swallowed, tried to quell the fluttering inside, told herself she had no need for nerves. But the moment before the door opened she had a second, a sliver of a second, when she thought she'd really rather die.

She pushed through, went in and it happened as it had all the last week. The large hand gripped her heart and squeezed, stopping the beat for two seconds too long, while lower in her belly someone switched on the heater.

He was in a suit. It was immaculate. He wasn't smiling.

But he was still brain-zappingly gorgeous and she was as bad as the thousand other women who fell at his feet—breathless, bedazzled. She tried to clear her mind of the clutter, to quell the hormones shrieking at her. Think Zen. Think power.

'Thanks, Kelly.'

Dani heard the door click. So it was shut. So they were alone.

He wasn't behind his desk; instead he stood on her side of it, in the middle of the room. 'My name is—'

'I know who you are.'

Their eyes met. His face was expressionless. But she knew he was remembering the moment after the last time she'd said that, just as she was. That time the spark in his eye had surprised her. The oh-so-relaxed boss, the charming playboy, had looked bitter for a half-second. She'd spent all that night wondering why—in between reliving the heat.

'Please sit down.' Quiet, firm and with that underlying note of authority.

Her legs moved towards the chairs without her instruction—just following his order. She seemed to have swallowed her tongue. Every sentence, the whole spiel she'd rehearsed as she'd steamed her way over here, had fled from her head. Mute, mindless, she was like some star-struck fan meeting her pin-up hottie in the flesh for the first time.

And then she saw it.

Every word, every angry thought, all of it came ripping back. She inhaled, trying to hold back enough to be able to tackle him with controlled fury rather than blind rage. Even so, she spat the words. 'Enjoying it?'

'What?'

'Your little home movie.' She pointed.

They were plastered across the screen. Her legs around his waist. Their tongues so entwined it was a wonder they'd ever managed to pull themselves free.

And he was watching it? Had spun the screen round so it was visible from right across the room?

As if the HR woman had just come to give him his warning—she'd come for a laugh, more like. Dani nearly choked on the rage that reddened her vision. Her face was so hot she was probably casting a glow into outer space. But that was nothing on the churning mass of fire in her belly. 'Why are you watching it?'

He hadn't known she was coming to see him. She'd only finally made her mind up as she'd walked past the building—had been regretting it all the five minutes since. She couldn't believe the whole nightmare. 'How did it happen?'

'What?' He took the seat next to hers. 'The kiss or the recording?' His mouth lifted at one end in a small smile.

She wasn't in the mood for seeing any kind of funny side—he wasn't going to defuse her with his attempt at good humour. 'The recording.'

'There are security cameras in all the lifts. Someone saw us, clipped the footage and put it up. As I think you know, it's been doing the rounds.'

'Yes, the viral video *du jour*,' she said bitterly. 'Was it a joke? Did you set it up for fun?'

'Of course not.' He went rigid. 'I'm the CEO of a large finance company. I think I have better things to do with my time than indulge in stupid pranks like this.'

He held her gaze a minute longer. Assessing. She withstood the scrutiny, tilting her chin that little higher. Refusing to be intimidated.

'Where have you been these last few days?' Assertive, that was how she'd be.

'Overseas.'

'How convenient for you—out of the country while the temp gets the boot and then can't find another job in the whole city.'

'What do you want me to do?'

'Give me my job back.'

He shook his head. 'Impossible.'

'How so?'

'You think you could sit there knowing they've all watched me kiss you like that?'

Kiss you. The words seemed to whisper over her skin, teasing her into greater awareness. She shifted in her seat, resettling her limbs in an attempt to stay in charge of them—and the whole nightmare. 'It was only a kiss, Mr Carlisle. It was nothing.' She shrugged.

His brows lifted for a second. 'You're not going back out there.'

Damn it, she *needed* this job. 'It was a moment. That's all it was. So some geek with nothing better to do made a mini movie with it. Not my fault.'

'You are not working on that floor again.'

'You're not understanding me. I need this job.'

'And I'm saying it's not going to happen.'

'Do you know what this is? Unfair dismissal. Sexual harassment.'

'That was not sexual harassment.' He pointed at the screen. 'You kissed me back. You wrapped your legs around me all by yourself.'

'But because of that video, I lost my job and I need my job. Because of that video, I can't get another. The world of recruitment agencies is really small here in Auckland, do you know that? The agents all know each other, all swap from company to company. And they send each other *emails*. Would you believe that?' Dani inhaled. 'That stupid kiss has cost me everything and I can't let it. How come you get to sit here in your fancy office and suffer none of the consequences while my life gets totalled?' She stood. 'It's not happening. This is unfair and I'll prove it's unfair. I'm going to a lawyer— see if you can say *"impossible"* to a court!'

She whirled and marched. She had no idea where to find a lawyer, whether she really did have a case, and she certainly didn't have the money to pay for it but she was bloody well going to find it somehow.

She opened the door but it was slammed shut again—his big hand spread wide on the wood above her head and firmly holding it in place.

'You don't shout at me and walk out without giving me a chance to respond.'

'Watch me.' She pulled on the door handle with all her strength. It didn't move.

'This is what happens. We talk. We negotiate. You're not leaving until you've let me think of an alternative.'

She turned to glare at him and discovered he was way too close. Right beside her, so all she could see was his body—

the jacket of his suit pulled wide by the way his arm was stretched out, revealing the breadth of his chest in the crisp white cotton beneath. His physicality was so potent, all she could feel was the warmth of him reaching out to her. The temptation to step closer was almost crippling—and totally wrong, wrong, wrong.

'What kind of alternative?' The woolly feeling was seeping into her head. She lifted her chin to be able to look into his face and the brain lethargy only worsened. His eyes were looking very green.

'Sit back down and I'll explain. If you want we can get my HR manager to sit in on the meeting.'

Reality returned with acute vividness. That cow? 'That won't be necessary.'

His lips twitched. 'My PA, then.'

Nope, not the boarding-school matron, either. 'Look, you and I both know that if you lay a hand on me, I'll be screaming the place down.'

His face suddenly lit up like a Christmas tree and his smile went so wicked she wouldn't have been surprised if he had a doorway to a den of sin hidden behind his desk. Or maybe that was wishful thinking—because when he looked like that all she could think about was bad, bad behaviour. Then she mentally replayed what she'd said and suddenly felt a need to clarify. 'Screaming in *horror*.'

'Ri-i-ight.' He nodded as if she were a delusional diva he had to humour. 'All outrage rather than ecstasy.'

She opened her mouth but before she'd thought of a comeback he'd lifted his hand from the door, and was holding it and the other up in the 'don't shoot' position, his mouth in a smile too cheeky to resist.

He'd be dead if her eyes had ammo. Sadly her eyes were

too busy gobbling up the gorgeousness before her to execute the death look. Her failing brain managed one last attempt to control the weakening of her body and she tried the door again. It still didn't move. She glanced down. His foot was jammed against it.

'I really have been overseas. I left the afternoon we were in the lift. The trip was unavoidable. I expected to see you when I got back. To talk to you.' His hands had dropped to his hips. She couldn't stop looking at his long fingers.

'What were you going to say?'

'It doesn't matter.' His fingers curled into fists. 'What matters is that I found out about the clip this morning and I found out about you being dismissed two minutes ago.'

She took a step back from the door so she could look into his face from a safer distance. 'You didn't know?' He hadn't ordered it?

'No. The clip was taken from the security camera in the lift. I don't know who did it yet, but when I find out you can be certain that *that* person will be in danger of dismissal.'

That sharp edge sliced back into his eyes for a second. She wanted it to stay—wanted him to truly understand the impact. 'It's had hundreds of hits. It got sent to the agency. I got a warning for it but by some great coincidence they can't complete the necessary verification on my paperwork.' Shaking her head, she walked into the middle of the room—the greater the distance between them, the better she could think.

'I know.'

'So what are you going to do?' It wasn't the unfairness of the ramifications that had brought her here, it was that she needed help and had nowhere else to turn. And she hated it.

'I'm not sure yet.'

That wasn't good enough. She spun and saw the wicked

smile was back on his face. He thought this was funny? He still didn't get how serious it was for her? She walked back to stand right in front of him, whipping the words out.

'Thanks to you I have no job and no hope of getting another one. Thanks to you I am flat broke. I'm in a strange country, I don't know anyone and suddenly I'm starring in some local sex clip and all you want to do is laugh it off.' Breathing hard, she glared at him—her eyes filled with the ammo they'd lacked before.

His grin was wiped. 'I don't think it's funny.'

'Oh, really? So that's why you're smiling like some satyr and watching replays like it's the joke of the century.'

'It wasn't a joke.' His eyes bored into hers so intently she couldn't move. His face hardened in the long seconds of silence. She sensed the rest of him becoming tense too—his body sending such strong vibes of tightly leashed energy that she could feel them pressing on her.

For a second her instinct screamed at her to run, but just as fast the urge was squashed. Other urges began to surge instead—and she needed a strong leash of her own to control them. Her whole body was aware of him, her whole focus was on him. His gaze dropped to her mouth and she felt it like a physical touch. He was remembering—as was she, and the fire arcing between them threatened to burn through her control. But she wasn't going to let this raging attraction muck up more of her life. She wasn't going to lose the little credibility she had left by letting it happen again.

She made her body move—away—a few steps back towards the door.

'You really can't get another job?' His voice sounded rusty.

'You really think I'd be here if I could?'

His brows drew closer as he regarded her. The angles of

his face became more pronounced. Suddenly, sharply, he moved. Walking to the window, he glared through it—she figured the glass would melt in moments if he still had that heat in his eyes.

'I might have another job for you. But not here. I don't think that's something you or I or anyone would be comfortable with.' He turned. It seemed he'd taken the time to ice over, for his face was schooled into blandness. 'Look, let's get out of here and go talk somewhere more relaxed.'

He opened the door and waited for her to pass through. Dani hesitated—relaxed might be a really bad idea. But if he could do cucumber cool, surely she could do better than melting jelly.

CHAPTER THREE

DANI kept three feet behind Alex as he strode past the PA.

'Please cancel that last appointment and take messages, Kelly. I'm out for the rest of the afternoon,' he said without slowing his pace.

'Certainly.' No surprise, no questions. The PA gave Dani a coolly professional smile but Dani was still too rattled to be able to match it.

Alex glanced at the lift. 'Shall we take the stairs?'

Dani was already at the door to them—hoped the PA hadn't heard his question. He'd laced it with the faintest hint of irony and if Dani were to look at him now and see him smiling she couldn't be held responsible for her actions—aggressive energy seemed to be bouncing round her body.

'Where are you staying?' He thudded downstairs swiping a security card to get them into the basement.

She gave him the name of the hostel and saw his frown appear.

'You don't know Auckland, do you?' He sent her a sideways glance. 'Because if you did, you'd know that's in a really dodgy part of town.'

It was a cheap part of town.

He unlocked the car—sleek, attractive, outrageously powerful, just like its owner. Dani got into the passenger seat. In seconds they were out of the garage and driving down the congested inner-city streets in awkward silence—he'd quickly cut the music that had roared louder than the engine. Dani wished he'd kept it on—better to listen to that than the silence between them or the voice in her head telling her how much of a mess she was in. The weather had turned, the rain drizzling and dampening her spirits further.

'Um…' he was drumming his fingers on the steering wheel '…I…'

Dani waited, surprised by his sudden attack of the fidgets.

His fingers abruptly stopped their beat and gripped the wheel. 'What's your name?'

'Pardon?'

'Your name.' He kept his eyes on the road ahead. 'I don't know what it is.'

'You don't know my name?' Stunned, Dani stared at him. 'How can you not know my name?'

'We never finished our introductions.' His high cheekbones were streaked with slashes of colour. 'I have a lot of employees.'

'Oh, and I was just one of the temps.' OK, so she was. But she hadn't been just one of them—he'd kissed the hell out of her. She'd *felt* him and he had her—*intimately*. Or did he do that with all the girls? Anger roared through her again—vicious, wild anger. 'You could have found out.'

'I don't use the HR files for personal reasons.'

'No, you just use the temps.'

He braked sharply at the traffic lights. 'I didn't use you and you know it.'

Dani shook her head, stupidly hurt by his admission. 'No, I don't.'

She wanted to get out of the car and away from him right this second. It was beyond humiliating—she'd gone to him because she had nowhere else to go for help, using her anger to mask the hope that he'd actually feel some kind of responsibility. Buried right beneath everything had been the teeny, tiny hope that he might have actually liked her. What a fool. The whole thing had been so meaningless for him that he hadn't even bothered to learn her name. He could have found out—his HR dragon or his oh-so-efficient PA could have told him. But he hadn't asked—he hadn't wanted to. So while she'd been blown away by that kiss, he hadn't given it a second thought, other than to be a little annoyed about the resulting clip—or perhaps amused was what he'd been. But the video didn't affect him the way it did her—all it did for him was enhance his reputation as some kind of playboy sex god. But for her it ruined everything—her prospects, her plans, *her* reputation. 'You know something, Mr Carlisle, I don't care how good a job you can offer me. I don't want it.'

'Look—'

'I'm serious. You can drop me at the corner.'

The locks in the car clicked on. She shot him a venomous look.

'I'll take you to the hostel.' He looked angry, which was so wrong because he was the one who had been insulting, not her.

They were almost at the hostel already—Dani recognised the landmarks. He must have intended to take her there anyway. So much for a conversation somewhere more relaxing—so much for the possibility of a different job.

She was out of the car as soon as he'd pulled over and released the locks, felt her tension yanking tighter when he got out of the car just as quick. 'You don't need to see me in.'

'The least I can do is see you safely home.' He glared at the hostel's sign, his frown saying all that he thought about her home—all that he thought about her.

Dani marched up the stairs ahead of him, wishing he'd get the hint and just leave. But he was right behind her as she crossed the floor.

'Excuse me,' the receptionist called out to her. 'Danielle Russo?'

Dani veered towards the desk. Alex got to the counter at the same time as her. So now he knew her name—way too late.

Dani lifted her brows at the woman behind the desk and managed an almost-smile—not able to trust that her voice wouldn't be razor sharp if she asked if there was a problem.

'We need you to pay for this week. It's nothing personal—but we have had trouble with people leaving without paying and then their credit-cards not working. And, er—' the receptionist looked at her notes '—we don't seem to have credit card details for you.'

That was because Dani knew all about credit cards not working—and, worse, being abused. 'I paid cash,' she mumbled.

'Great. Shall we settle it now, then?'

Dani swallowed. 'I already paid for last week.'

'I know.' She looked apologetic. 'But I now need payment for this week.'

Alex was like a statue next to her, listening to every word of the painful exchange. Could the day get any worse? Did he really have to be here to witness this last painful humiliation?

'Um.' Dani mumbled some more. 'I'm waiting on my pay before I can do the next week.'

'Oh.' The receptionist frowned and then suddenly smiled. 'Well, what about you pay up to tonight, then, and you can pay the rest tomorrow.'

'Sure.' Dani nodded. 'Thank you.' There was no pay tomorrow. All she had was in her bag—the two days' wages she'd got from the agency this morning. She felt her face on fire, felt the sweat trickling down her back as she handed over most of her last dollars.

Nightmare.

She turned and saw him watching her closely, his expression serious. Had he seen the lack of notes in her purse? Her anger spiked again—what was he going to do, pull out his fat wallet and hand over a couple of hundred to her? The humiliating thing was, much as she wanted to, she wouldn't be able to refuse. She hated being backed into a corner like this. While she needed help, her pride didn't want to take a thing from him. She wanted him to leave. Now. Bitter tears stung her eyes and she blinked them away, trying to build up her defences again—getting emotional only made things a million times worse. Getting emotional made you vulnerable.

'Thank you for dropping me back to the hostel,' she said fiercely. 'I'm sorry I bothered you at work. Let's just forget the whole thing, shall we?'

Alex watched her go—head high, shoulders back—but it was more of a run than a walk. He hesitated for half a second, then strode straight after her. Damn it, he couldn't just leave her so obviously on the skids. He walked into the dorm room she'd turned into. His skin crawled when he saw the state of it; what a dump.

'What are you doing in here?' She was standing by the bunks, her hands visibly shaking. As he glanced at her she screwed them into fists. No, she didn't want him to see her distress. He looked about the hideous room to give her a second, feeling like rubbish himself. Her pack was open on the bottom bunk. His eyes flicked over the gloriously huge bra poking out the top and quickly he turned his back on that. He glanced back at her—now she was watching him as if she wanted to beat the hell out of him.

OK, this was bad. Really bad. She was living in a dodgy part of town in a flea-infested hostel in a room with a bunch of strangers. And she was about to be turfed out of it. He felt terrible. He felt responsible. And this was the last thing he needed—he already had enough mess cluttering up his mind. So he had to do something—anything—to fix it. 'Danielle.'

Her eyes narrowed.

'I heard the receptionist.' He shrugged. It was a pretty name. He wished he'd known it sooner. 'Put your things together.'

'Pardon?'

'You can't stay here.' It just wasn't going to happen.

'Yes, I can. Look, I was wrong to interrupt you today. *I* made a mistake the other day. I can live with the consequences.'

'Well, I can't.' He took a step closer. 'Gather your things together and we'll find you someplace else to stay.'

'Where?'

He clamped his mouth shut. Yeah—where? Was he going to put her up in a hotel or something? For how long? Think, brain, think. Where were the solutions to problems that he usually found so easily? But he couldn't think because he was still seeing the lace edging of that pretty white bra and the play part of his head was imagining what it would look like on her. 'Someplace else.'

'I can't afford anywhere else.'

Yeah, and she couldn't afford here, either, could she? He could offer her money. Lots of money. Wouldn't that make it all go away? Why the hell hadn't he just written her a cheque in his office?

Because Alex hadn't got to the top without dotting 'i's and crossing 't's—Alex never left a job unfinished. He needed to make sure she really was back on her feet. She couldn't get a job—there were no jobs. He knew this—his HR department had got over a hundred applicants for the single permanent position they'd advertised. For her to have got the temp position meant her references and skills were brilliant. The personal issue between them had blown it. So he owed her.

But what made him determined to truly see for himself that she was OK was the expression he'd seen—the vulnerability in the elevator. In those brief moments when the façade had dropped, he'd seen the fear in her eyes. And he'd seen it again at the counter of the hostel. She was isolated and alone.

The protective male bit in him dominated the direction of his thoughts. 'Do you have any friends here?'

The answer was obvious and she didn't even bother voicing it.

'Do you know *anyone*?'

Her chin lifted. 'I only arrived in the country two weeks ago and got straight to work the minute I could. Sadly I didn't have the time to make friends there.' She got in a little dig.

Why was she in New Zealand anyway? He turned; there was time to find that out later. What mattered now was settling her in someplace else. Someplace safer. 'Let's go.'

'I'm not leaving here with you. I'm fine.' Her feet were firmly planted shoulder width apart; she looked as if she was about to declare that he'd have to carry her out forcibly.

And he felt like it. But instead of obeying the urge of his body, he softened his words with a smile. 'Face it, Danielle, you don't really have a choice. You're not getting paid tomorrow because you got paid when you left the agency. You could only pay for one more night here. You have no money, no friends to call on. And you're obviously not fine, because if you were you never would have been so worked up that you had to come and see me today.'

Her eyes were huge in her face now. He saw her blinking

fast a couple of times and gentled his tone even more. 'Get your things. I'll take you to a hotel or something.'

For another long moment he thought she was going to refuse. But then he saw her swallow and turn, bending to pull her pack from the bed. He moved to help her but was lanced through with her glare.

His lips twitched but he managed to bite back the smile as he froze. She had to accept his help anyway and she hated it. She'd hate him more if he showed his amusement. So he looked away, checking the cupboard beside her bed was bare. Just as he turned to go he caught sight of something under the bunk, and bent to see what it was. A little candle, deep red in colour and new—the tip of the wick was still white. He picked it up and sniffed. The fragrance was delectable. Edible.

'This yours?' He held it out as she turned, the pack now on her back.

Soft colour rose in her cheeks. Interesting.

'Yes,' she answered shortly and took it from him.

Alex watched her tuck it into the pocket of her handbag. So beneath the snappy defensiveness there was a feminine side—she liked pretty candles with sweet smells. The kind of scent he could handle in his sheets.

No, Alex.

His moment of irresponsibility in the lift last week had caused her trouble enough already. She might be attractive, but he wasn't going to mess around with her more. He'd see her right and then run far, far away. He had enough to deal with without lust fogging up his brain—and that was exactly what was happening every minute he was near her. The fog blurred everything—especially his reason. So the sooner he had her sorted, the better it would be, because he had far bigger issues to stomach.

He glanced at his watch, surprised to see how late in the afternoon it was. Lorenzo would be waiting for him. He might as well take her home and figure out what to do from there.

Dani watched the sky-high metal gates in front of them roll back and then Alex drove the car into the garage. Only once the engine and his seat belt were off did he look at her, brows lifting. 'Safe at last.'

Oh, yeah. Real safe. She listened as the heavy garage door sealed shut. So here she was in Fort Knox with the guy she barely knew but who had all but ravished her in the lift last week. And she'd let him. Really, really safe.

He was wearing that far-too-wide smile again. 'Come on, Danielle. Let's go sort this out.'

'This isn't a hotel.'

'No.'

'This is your house.'

'Yes.'

'This isn't a good idea.'

'Relax.' He led the way up the short flight of stairs. 'I want to find a solution to this mess just as much as you do. Here we can do that in privacy.'

'Is there really a job?'

'Danielle—'

'Dani,' she snapped, unable to bear hearing her full name a second longer. She hadn't been Danielle in years. She was Dani. Her tomboy name—keeping her sexless and uninteresting to her mother's boyfriends, until puberty had really hit and her body had let her down. Then she'd had to go for more forceful tactics.

'Dani,' he repeated, smile vanishing.

She regretted correcting him. When he said it with his

rounder New Zealand vowels it sounded so much smoother. The tingle went in her ears all the way down her centre to her toes—causing them to squirm restlessly in their boots.

'Everything OK?' Someone else spoke—with more than a hint of dryness.

Dani craned her head round Alex. There was another tall guy waiting for them at the top. So much for privacy.

'It will be.' Alex climbed the last of the stairs.

'It better be.' Dani followed him up into the room, determined to master her chaotic emotions. 'Who are you?'

'Lorenzo,' he answered as bluntly as she'd asked.

'Do you live here?' She couldn't keep the challenge out of her voice—it was the way she'd always hidden her fear.

A glance passed between the two men. Lorenzo took a step towards the stairs. 'I'm guessing we'll talk later.'

'No, I want you to meet Dani,' Alex said so smoothly that Lorenzo paused and looked. 'She's going to take over when Cara goes on maternity leave.'

Lorenzo's mouth opened, but then shut.

'Full-time position, of course, but starting from now,' Alex added.

Dani darted looks between Alex and Lorenzo—saw Lorenzo's eyes had widened slightly, but still he said nothing.

'You'll get Cara to show her what to do.' Alex was telling, not asking.

'Absolutely. No problem.' Lorenzo's impassivity shattered with a smile. 'And as Dani is obviously staying here with you, you can drop her to the warehouse tomorrow.'

Alex's eyes were the ones widening now.

'Talk more later, Alex,' Lorenzo said.

'Yep.' It was amazing sound could emerge from the mask his face had become.

Lorenzo looked at Dani and then at Alex again, his smile turning into a total smirk. 'Nice to meet you, Dani. See you tomorrow.'

CHAPTER FOUR

DANI waited 'til he'd gone down the stairs and she'd heard the door shut after him. Then she turned to Alex. 'What job?' She'd deal with the most palatable issue first.

'Administrator for the Whistle Fund.'

The charitable fund his company supported. Alex was on the board. She knew this from his fangirl at the water-cooler.

'Lorenzo is the chief exec. The organisation is based in his building. Cara, the current administrator, is pregnant and needs some help.'

'And it's a paid position? Full-time?' She'd always thought these kind of jobs were voluntary—wealthy wives doing some part-time hours for fun and fulfilment.

'Yes.'

Dani thought. 'I've done numbers more than admin.'

'Which is perfect, because this is all about dealing with money and there's a huge overlap in terms of dealing with systems for paperwork. And there's probably more variety. You'd be taking lots of calls, answering queries, sending out info packs, sorting the requests, updating the Web site. I'm sure you can manage a phone and talk nice to people.'

She'd started as a teller. She liked the interaction with the public—more so than the back-room dealing with the corporate banking she'd gone into.

'Cara really does need help.' His persuasion continued. 'You're good at your job. I'm sure you'll pick it up, no problem.'

'How do you know I'm good at my job when you didn't even know my name?' She couldn't resist sticking a pin in his smooth-talking bubble.

'We only recruit exceptional employees—even temporary workers have to be of Carlisle standard.'

Carlisle standard? Oh, he had an answer for everything. And what was the bet he had a standard in bed too? If it was anything like his kissing standard it wouldn't just be exceptional, it would be nothing short of spectacular. But it wasn't helpful to think about that now. She took a step back towards the stairs.

'Why don't you do a week's trial?' He was relentless, taking a step after her—not letting her increase her distance from him.

OK, so she really didn't have a choice. But she had to admit she was actually interested to see what it was like too. 'OK,' she answered, crossing her fingers that this wasn't a huge mistake. 'Thanks.'

He smiled then. 'Now that's sorted, come on through and have a drink.'

He was walking off before she could refuse. And she couldn't refuse, could she—couldn't be completely rude—not now he'd given her a job?

The town house was gorgeous—a traditional wooden villa on the outside but one that had been rebuilt on the inside. High ceilings and big windows let in lots of light. Neutral but warm colours made it welcoming. A huge painting hung on the wall above the fireplace. The lounge was big and the sofa comfortable-looking. But she didn't sit, instead she walked to the window and saw the last of the sun's light was turning the clouds a fiery orange. She was unfamiliar with the geography of Auckland, but somehow she'd expected a view of the city buildings, or perhaps the water. She wasn't expecting the verdant, lush garden. It was like a miniature forest. So gorgeously green in the middle of winter and so private.

'Can I get you a drink?'

She turned her back on the beauty of it. 'No, thanks.'

He didn't get himself one, either, just stood on the far side of the long, low coffee table by the sofa. 'Take a seat, Dani.'

'I don't feel comfortable about staying here.'

'Why not?'

She opened her mouth and then shut it again.

'You're no longer working for me. Technically Lorenzo will be your boss.' With wide-spread fingers, he ruffled through his hair, rubbing his head hard. He closed his eyes for a second. 'I'm sorry, OK?'

Oh, it was hours too late for the repentant-man act. She wasn't falling for it. 'Maybe next time you should try keeping your hormones in check. What was it all about anyway? Kiss-a-temp day?'

'You misunderstand.' His eyes shot open, lancing through her. 'I'm not sorry I kissed you. I'll never regret that experience. It would be an insult to you if I did.'

'Oh, please.' Too smooth. Way too smooth. And the sparkling humour in his unwavering gaze just made her want to tell him so. But, damn, her cheeks were burning—she must look like a totally floored teen. So embarrassing.

His scrutiny intensified. 'What I'm sorry about is the whole office watching, and the gossip.'

'I don't care about the gossip. People can think what they like—it makes no difference to me.'

His brows flickered but he didn't question. 'Fair enough,

but I care about it and I won't have either you or me on the line because of it. I'm sorry about what the agency did. This will make it right.' He sighed, jammed his hands in his pockets. 'Where's your family—in Australia?'

'I don't have any. My parents are dead,' she said baldly.

'I'm sorry.' His frown deepened.

Instantly she regretted telling him—she didn't want his pity, but more than that she didn't want to remember. The lump in her chest when she thought of her mother was like sharp, burning ice and she hurriedly turned her thoughts away from her. But not to her father—as far as she was concerned he'd never been alive to her. Instead she pushed the focus back onto Alex, remembering what she'd been told. 'Your father died last year.'

Silence. She'd hit a nerve. His frown disappeared as his face smoothed, then it shuttered completely into unreadable blandness. 'You're up on your research.'

'You were the number-one topic of conversation at the water-cooler.' She aimed for flippant, trying to cover the moment of awkwardness. 'I didn't even have to ask.'

A slight grin reappeared. 'But you were going to? You wanted to find out?'

'No. It was all thrust upon me.'

His low laughter refreshed the room, lightening everything—including her mood. She even grinned back.

He immediately pressed his argument home. 'Look, I'm hardly here. I travel a lot. It would be good to have someone minding the house. You can stay for a week or two and save some money to get into a place of your own. It's the simplest solution. We'll hardly see each other.'

Dani considered it. What was she so worried about—her unreal attraction to him? If he was away a lot, then she could control it, right? And it wasn't as if he were trying to pounce again. He might have said he didn't regret kissing her, but neither had he asked for another. It was a bit deflating, but it seemed all he felt for her now was a sense of responsibility—not unbridled lust. She wouldn't misinterpret his charm as meaning something more.

His brows lifted fractionally, as if he knew he'd won. 'So it's a deal.' He held out his hand.

Dani looked at it. Surely she had nothing to lose and everything to gain. She could work, not worry about a roof over her head and be able to find Eli.

But, like that day in the lift, her instinct was warning her again, that sense of impending danger. She ignored it and reached out. 'Thanks.'

The spark shot up her arm. His fingers tightened. And she realised her instinct had been bang on the money. She shouldn't have touched him. *He* was the danger—his attraction too magnetic. He made her body go on edge in an entirely new way.

'Don't you want to know, Dani?' The warmth from his whisper flooded her.

'Know what?' She beat the breathlessness with assertion.

'What would have happened if we hadn't been caught on camera? What would have been the next step?'

'There wouldn't have been a next step. I've already told you, it was a moment. Nothing more.'

'You're sure about that?' He kept hold of her hand but took the two steps around the coffee table between them. 'See, I think there would have been a next step, Dani. A very pleasurable one.'

Oh, hell. So it wasn't just her feeling it. But she held her ground. 'I'm sorry to disappoint you, Alex, but I'm not going to be your next lover.'

'No?' His eyes danced.

'No.' She smiled sweetly. 'I'm going to be your flatmate. And there's a rule about flatmates, isn't there?' *Don't screw the crew.*

His smile was reluctant but it was there. She took the chance to tug her hand from his. Even so, the victory was hollow. Now she knew she couldn't possibly stay here, for she'd lied—she desperately wanted to know what would have happened next. But she figured she could get him to change his mind and hustle her into a hotel pronto. 'Aren't I going to cramp your style?'

'How so?'

'Who did you go out with last Friday night?'

'No one.' He shrugged. 'I was in Sydney working.'

'OK.' Dani frowned. 'What about the one before that?'

His hesitation was telling.

'A woman. Obviously,' Dani said, her voice as melted-chocolate smooth as his had been before.

Slowly he nodded.

'And the Friday before that?' Dani enquired. 'A different woman, right?'

He squared his stance, facing her full on. 'Yes.'

'And you slept with them.' Still calm, determinedly not judging.

'No.'

That made her pause a moment. 'Kissed them good-night, at least.'

'Yes.'

Yeah. She knew what his kisses were like. 'So isn't it going to be tricky for you to bring a woman home when you have me staying here?' She let a touch of taunt out then. She had to get him to realise sticking her in a hotel was a much better option. The prospect of staying in close confines with him made her feel giddy—she wasn't sure she could keep her need-to-shimmy urges under control.

'You know, you're right.' He had a devilish look on his face. 'It might be a bit weird to bring dates home while having you as my little flatmate here. But that's no problem.' He paused, and she swore she could see the wickedness rippling through the rest of him as he stepped closer. 'You can be my date while you're staying here.'

'What?'

'There are a few things I have to go to and, you're right, I like a companion. No reason why that can't be you.'

She opened her mouth but he put a finger on it.

'There isn't anyone else around right now anyway.' His green eyes bored into hers as he oh-so-unsubtly let her know he was available.

'Not this week, you mean.' So there damn well shouldn't be or he shouldn't have kissed her like that.

'So you can stay here and save, just for a week or two.' He ignored her hit. 'Until you're in a position to take a place of your own. Meantime I have a dinner to go to tomorrow night—very nice venue, black tie. Don't you love a little glamour?'

'No.' She threw him a dark look, trying to keep a grip on herself. This wasn't what she'd meant to happen. He hadn't even bothered to learn her name—she needed to keep that little fact up front and centre in her head.

'I thought all women did.'

'Not me.'

'Oh.' He smiled. 'I'll have to help you change your mind on that. Dances like this one can be a lot of fun.'

'I thought you said it was a dinner.'

'Followed by dancing.' He looked thoughtful. 'Have you

got something to wear?' He ignored her start of annoyance. 'We can go shopping tomorrow afternoon if you'd like.'

Go shopping? 'You don't need to *Pretty Woman* me, Alex,' she said sharply. 'I have something to wear.'

'Great, that's settled, then.' He turned away flashing a Cheshire Cat smile, then turned back just as quick. 'Oh…'

'What?' Rattled, she snapped—had she just agreed to go out with him tomorrow night? How had that happened?

'What about you?' With that too-bland expression he moved back into her space. 'Who did you go out with last Friday night?'

'I—' She blinked. No one, of course.

'What about the Friday before? Is there a boyfriend I ought to know about? I mean, you asked me, I can ask you, right? I don't want to put you in a difficult position as my escort.'

Escort was not a good word—the unpleasant connotation compounded with his offer to take her shopping pushed her defence button. She wasn't anybody's paid-for plaything. She'd prefer to be the player, not the toy.

'Of course you won't.' She lifted her chin and fired a shot at him. 'I don't do "boyfriends" as such, but I have a few joy boys around. I choose one to service me occasionally but we share nothing more than that. *Variety*,' she added with a con-spiratorial whisper. 'You know.' She was quite sure he did know. Quite sure he had a whole variety line-up of lovers himself—only his wouldn't be imaginary.

'Occasionally?' His brows lifted. 'Only occasionally?' His smile was feral. 'No wonder you burned so hot in my arms.'

She opened her mouth to snap at him but this time he laid his whole hand across her mouth, leaning in to quiz her. 'You don't believe in romance?'

She pulled back from the sizzling touch. 'I don't believe

in romance, relationships or anything like that. I certainly don't believe in marriage.'

'A free woman?'

'Absolutely,' she declared. 'An independent one.' Her aim was to take only what she wanted when she wanted and leave the rest of the rubbish for others to suffer through. Except she'd not really managed it yet and now wasn't the time to start trying. She had something way more important to be focused on. It had taken her long enough to earn back the money her father had stolen, and truthfully she'd come over too soon—without all she should have. So she didn't need distractions now—not of any kind.

He stepped even closer, gleaming green eyes trained on her. 'Don't you believe it can happen, Dani? A look across a room? Love at first sight?'

'Never in a million years.' She straightened her shoulders. 'And you don't, either.' The man was a complete playboy. But he had every right to be—he had every necessary asset: the looks, the humour, the drive.

'No,' he agreed, looking her over, top to toe and back again so every inch of her skin was sizzling. 'Not love. But lust is another matter.' He tilted his head as if to study her from a different angle. 'Why are you breathing so hard? Something bothering you?'

'I don't like confined spaces.' Hell, he got to her.

'I know the house isn't huge, but it's not exactly tiny.'

It wasn't tiny at all. She stared into his green eyes. 'I don't like feeling trapped.'

'You're not trapped,' he said calmly, then moved fast, his arms hauling her to him. 'But now you are.'

She twisted in his embrace. 'Watch it, I've a black belt in Tae Kwon Do.'

'Really?'

His muscles tightened—catching her, stopping her. It felt appallingly good. She twisted again, only succeeded in pressing her breasts even harder against his chest. Her nipples screamed with sensitivity. 'OK, no. But I have done self-defence classes.' She tried to twist free one more time.

'Let me guess—practising against other women, right?'

Damn. She fought harder. But he must have had some kind of fighter training too. It couldn't just be his sheer strength stopping her. Oh, hell, the adrenalin surged through her—excitement, challenge, anticipation. She summoned her strength back up.

'I don't think you should do that again.' He grunted as she hit out with her leg.

'Why not?' Panting, she sent him a death look.

'Because all you're doing is turning me on.' Goaded, he pushed her from him. 'And you're turned on too. You're aching for it, just like I am.'

Breathless, she stared, mouth falling at his arrogant certainty. But standing with her feet planted shoulder-width apart, she felt it, the flood of juices that would make his entry slick, the softening within her. He was right, so right.

She bit down on her lips. Wanting and angrily not wanting to want. Her teeth seemed to sharpen. Every muscle primed. She could howl with the need.

'You want to fight for it? You like it fast and hard? 'Cause I can do that. I can do that right now,' he growled. 'But tell me, who is it you're really fighting, Dani? Is it me or is it yourself?'

She gasped. 'You arrogant jerk.'

'Yeah.' His laugh was rough. 'But it's just sex. It's just fun.' He walked towards her again. 'You already know how incredible we'd be.'

It was surprisingly easy to fell a full-grown man—but she did have the element of surprise. A quick kick with her leg tripped him and sent him to the floor. But he was faster—his hand catching her ankle before she could dodge back to a safe distance. He pulled. The breath knocked from her lungs as she thudded down on top of him. He rolled, spinning her over and pinning her half under him. He was heavy. Hard. The shiver ran through her whole body. His body flexed in response.

Their eyes met.

'I could beat you if I wanted to,' she said, wincing at her breathlessness.

'I'm sure you could. *If* you wanted to.' His hand swept down her side.

'Get off. You're heavy.' She wasn't in the least afraid, but she was desperate to deny the way her body was softening—the way her bones were melting with need.

'Oh…no…' he said slowly, brushing her hair from her eyes with gentle fingers before putting his hand on her hip. 'I don't want to.'

'I want you to.'

'Do you?' He stroked up the side of her body, his hand gently sweeping up to cup her breast, his thumb caressing the stiff peak. 'You don't want to do anything about this?'

She didn't play dumb and ask what he meant. Instead she chomped on the urge to arch her back so it would press her nipple harder against the palm of his hand. And she pleaded with her hips to stay still and not rock that little bit more into his hardness. She dug her fingers into the carpet. The heat was stifling—it wasn't the weight of him hindering her breathing, it was the searing temperature between them.

Their eyes held, vision intensifying. Every inch of her body loved the feel of him, but her head was hurting.

'It would be a really bad idea,' she whispered. She lowered her lashes so she wouldn't drown in his eyes and say something she'd regret. 'My life is complicated enough right now.'

There was a long moment of silence when they were utterly motionless, both straining against the delicious torture of temptation.

'Yeah,' finally he groaned. 'So is mine.' He rolled and stood in the one movement. Shook his head as he looked down at her. 'I'll stay away.' Then he walked—fast—as if to emphasise it. 'I'll get your bag.'

Dani scrambled to her feet as soon as he was gone. Smoothed her hands down her flaming cheeks, tried to get her grip back and shake off the stab of disappointment. Unbelievable. She'd been so close to surrendering everything just then. But she'd spoken the truth—her life was complicated enough. And messing around with a guy like Alex would only make that worse. Despite what she'd said, she wasn't a player. She needed to stay on the sidelines.

He returned a few minutes later, lugging her pack, didn't look at her as he spoke. 'I'll show you to your room.' He led the way up another flight of stairs, stopping at an open door.

'This is your bedroom. You have a bathroom through that door.' He nodded towards the far corner of the room.

'Where's your bedroom?'

The corner of his mouth tilted up. 'You want to see it?'

'No, I just want to ensure it's far, far from mine.' She was only half kidding.

'This is only a two-bedroom town house, sweetheart. Mine is just up those stairs there.'

So he'd be sleeping above her. She was not thinking the naughty about that.

'There's a pretty high-tech security system I switch on at

night,' he said. 'If you go outside, you'll set off all the alarms. Even the balcony.'

'Are you telling me I'm a prisoner in here?'

'No. I'm telling you that if you go outside, you'll set off all the alarms. If you want to go out you can, just call out to me first and I'll disarm them.'

She relaxed a smidge. 'I won't want to go out.'

'Great.'

He moved into her room and she followed, looking about at the light walls and rich coverings on the fantastically huge bed. She didn't expect him to just drop the bags and turn so that she nearly bumped into him.

They both made like statues.

Except on the inside Dani's vital organs were at war—her brain was shutting down while her heart was pumping faster than the pistons in a Formula One racing car.

When he was close like this all she could think about was kissing him again—and doing a whole lot more. *Why don't you?* The little imp whispered inside her head.

Dani looked into his widened green eyes, teetering on losing herself in their mesmerising depths. He was so close and so aware.

Why didn't she? Because it would be too easy. And Dani had never been one to take the easy option. She would never *be* the easy option—for all her tarty talk to him. A simple few minutes now would mean complicated mess later—that she did know. She was her mother's daughter—susceptible to over-emotionality and that spelt weakness. Time after time she'd seen her mother's softness used against her. And when Dani had finally opened up to someone, she'd been trodden over too. Independence and clear-headedness was all—she needed to reclaim both right now.

The defence Dani had learned was to challenge, to say something smart, even issue a sting. But only millimetres from Alex, it was taking everything she had to stay in control. That made her nervous—and in turn that increased her determination to succeed. Her body went even more rigid.

One, then two, long seconds passed. His mouth was clamped shut and his eyes narrowed. Then he laced his fingers together, put them on his head as if he were an apprehended offender, and stalked from the room.

CHAPTER FIVE

DANI dragged herself from bed—having got to sleep only when the birds started their pre-dawn 'say hello to each other' chatter. She tugged up the trousers of her flannelette pyjamas and thudded down the stairs in search of coffee.

Newspapers were scattered all over the breakfast table and the radio was blaring. Dani blinked, struggling to adjust to the light, all the activity and the smell of fresh cooking. Alex was dressed in another devastating suit, sitting at the table with a giant glass of juice and halfway through demolishing an omelette already.

He paused, his fork halfway to his mouth as he looked her over. Dani held her head high—OK, the pink-pig-stamped pjs were indefensible, but at least they weren't sexy.

'You want one?' he asked. 'Won't take me a minute to whip it up.'

'No, thanks.' She turned her back on his blistering brightness. The words *want one* and *whip it up* coming from his mouth made her thoughts go squirmingly naughty.

'Not a morning person?'

Not when the night had been so long and she hadn't had her necessary six solid hours and a couple more in the doze-zone. She hadn't been able to move on from the doze-zone.

Because the semi-conscious dreams she'd had there had been rampantly X-rated and out of control. So, no, she wasn't a *this* morning person.

He made a small movement and the radio went silent. 'What about cereal? There's a selection in the pantry there.'

'Got coffee?'

He stood. 'How strong?'

'As strong as you've got.'

Dani looked at the pantry while he pushed buttons and got the oversized coffee contraption working. The pantry was oversized too—not just a cupboard you opened and filled the shelves of, but a small room that you could actually walk into—complete with its own butler's sink and small bench space. But despite her wanting to explore all the interesting-looking packs of foodie things on the shelves the space was just that bit too confined for her to feel comfortable. She walked out and inhaled.

'Nothing you like the look of?' Alex noted her empty hands.

Dani picked up the steaming mug he'd put on the table for her and told herself that there were plenty of other things in the whole entire world to like the look of. Not just Alex Carlisle.

'My housekeeper will get whatever you like in for you—just leave a note on the fridge.'

'Housekeeper?'

He nodded. 'Cleans, launders, cooks meals and is utterly discreet.'

Dani sank into a chair. 'The last being the most important, huh?'

Alex's brows lifted. 'You definitely need food.'

Dani just took another deep swig from the mug and closed her eyes as she swallowed the burning brain fuel. When she returned to almost-alive land Alex was at work behind the bench. There was a popping sound and he put two halves of a hot toasted bagel on the plate in front of him. He spread a thick layer of cream cheese onto it and several strips of smoked salmon on top of that. He put the finished plate of perfection in front of her.

OK, so that was something else to like the look of.

He nudged the plate closer. 'It's for eating.'

'Yeah. Thanks.' And it tasted almost as good as she figured he would.

He sat in the chair next to her and reached for his glass of juice, pulling part of the newspaper closer to read. 'Do you want me to organise a stylist for tonight?'

'A *what*?' She nearly choked on the bit of bagel.

'You know, someone to fix your hair and make-up?'

He thought she needed someone to fix her hair and make-up? Why? Didn't she make 'Carlisle standard'? Dani shrivelled inside as his words sliced right through her superficial layer of confidence. So she wasn't good enough to be seen out with at one of his posh fundraisers? She wasn't pretty or polished enough? Hurt, she put the bagel down, her appetite all gone. 'Are you sure you want me to come with you tonight?' She shrivelled more—hoped he hadn't heard her insecure edge.

Alex turned quickly to look at her, a frown drawing his brows together. Dani didn't look back at him, couldn't, was too flattened by his offer.

'Dani,' he said deliberately. 'There's nothing I want more than for you to come with me tonight. But I did promise I'd go to the dinner. And I don't want an empty chair beside me.' He put his hand on hers to stop her leaving the table.

She ignored her sizzling skin and gave him a baleful look. 'That wasn't what I meant.'

'I know you didn't,' he said, the cheeky grin giving way to

an earnest expression. 'Look, my mother never used to leave the house without having checked her appearance with her stylist. It's just something I'm used to. Not a comment on the way you look.'

A personal stylist? Wow—rich people like him really lived in an alternative universe, didn't they? But she didn't want to get sucked into the fantasy and start thinking such things were normal. She didn't want to be sucked in by Alex Carlisle any more than she'd been since she first clapped eyes on him.

'Umm, I think I can manage. It's only hair, right?' She cleared her throat, trying to get rid of the wounded rasp. 'And my style you can't do a lot with.' It was so thick she had to have it cut regularly into a plain and simple bob. But it was well overdue now, her fringe annoyingly long and too unruly for her to risk trimming herself—another reason to earn money asap.

He brushed the stupidly long bit back with his free hand and smiled, his gaze dropping to her pink pyjamas. Her toes curled into the heated tiles beneath her feet. What was she doing without shoes? And what was he doing looking so fine in his dark suit so early? And so clean-shaven? It was too early for that—shouldn't he be tousled, shouldn't his eyes be shadowed and sleepy, shouldn't he be…in bed?

'I'd better get ready.' She jerked up. 'Don't want to be late on my first day.'

The warehouse was impressive. Turned out Lorenzo was some sort of wine god and there were pallets of cases everywhere. And a very flash reception area and even a tasting room. Not that Alex stopped to give her the guided tour.

'The office is on the first floor.' He headed straight up. 'Cara, this is Dani.'

The woman behind the desk gave Dani a wide smile. Dani

registered the russet-coloured cropped hair and the elfin features and sparkling eyes.

'I'll leave you to it.' Alex was crisp. 'Take care of her.'

Dani wasn't sure who he meant by that—but he was gone before she could check.

'It'll be great to have you onboard,' Cara said cheerfully. 'There's always way too much to do.'

There was too. Dani's head whirled as she followed Cara through the routine. The woman was a dynamo—full of energy, effervescence and unfailing good humour.

She took the seat beside her and shadowed her while Cara explained everything in minute detail. It was fascinating and full on. But there was one burning question Dani couldn't bring herself to ask—how pregnant was Cara? Because her tummy was really, really flat. In fact, her tummy was flatter than Dani's. But she wasn't going to go personal—not on her first day. She was just here to work and pick up the wages.

Alex checked his watch again. He'd been stuck behind his desk for hours—hadn't gone down to the floor. No point. She wasn't there.

He should be feeling great. The situation with Dani was resolved, right? Now he could concentrate on far more important matters—like figuring out what he was going to do, whether he had any real right to be the boss at the bank. But his brain was stuck on one track. If he so much as thought of her his body went rock-hard. The things he wanted to do…but he hadn't taken her to his home to jump her bones the minute he had the chance, except the ache in his body had made him make moves and he'd loved every moment of touch and tease between them.

So had she. She couldn't deny the heat in her gaze, the reaction of her body—and she hadn't tried to. But she didn't want to act on it. And that got him.

He could kind of understand it. Her life was messed up enough—and in large part because of him. So succumbing to the lust—seducing her—just wasn't on, even though he knew it wouldn't take much to make it happen. But while Alex liked to play, he wanted an equally enthusiastic playmate.

Until she stepped up to the plate, he was standing back.

And she was a flatmate now, right? He knew the rule as well as she did—*don't screw the crew*. The one everyone learnt while flatting at university. Alex didn't mess around at work, and he sure as hell wasn't messing with someone in his own home.

He really shouldn't have taken her back there.

His phone rang, he glanced at the caller ID and congratulated himself on programming Patrick's mobile number in, because, nope, he was not answering. Alex wasn't ready to talk to him—maybe wouldn't ever be. What did the man expect—that he could back walk into his life, say, 'Hey, by the way, I'm your father, let's be friends.' As far as Alex was concerned, Patrick could stay in Singapore, where he had his luxury pad, a zillion servants and even more women. And if his conscience had started to prick him, too bad. Alex had no intention of making it easy for him. He took in a deep breath. He was too angry and he'd really rather channel that energy elsewhere.

He toyed with his pen and wondered what she was doing. He didn't like not being able to check on her. But Lorenzo could. Alex tossed the pen down as he realised he didn't like that, either. Lorenzo was a good-looking guy. Lorenzo liked women. And they liked him more.

He picked up the phone. His buddy-suddenly-turned-nemesis answered after one ring.

'How's she doing?' Alex skipped the preliminaries.

'I don't know. Fine, I'm sure.'

Alex frowned and spun his chair to look out the window—he could see the warehouse in the distance. 'Haven't you been to check?'

'I've got work to do so, no, I haven't. Do you want me to put you through to her phone?'

'No.' Silence. But Alex couldn't let it go yet. 'Why haven't you been to check?'

'What do you think I am—stupid?' Lorenzo grumbled. 'I'm not going anywhere near my best friend's latest lover.'

'She's not my lover.'

'Only a matter of time. Minutes. A few hours at the most.' Lorenzo chuckled. 'Breathe easy, brother.'

Alex sighed, then puffed out a smidge of amusement. 'Sorry.' They had never competed over a woman—had never had to given they went for totally different types. And until this second Alex had thought he'd walk away from any woman who threatened to come between him and Lorenzo—no hesitation. But Dani was different. The lust he felt for her made him want to fight his closest friend—the need was that sharp. But it seemed Lorenzo knew him better than he knew himself and was keeping far, far away.

So he could breathe easy? Yeah, as if that were possible when he had temptation-on-legs living in his town house and a bad case of honour afflicting him.

For the first time in ages he left the office for lunch—wandered down to the little exclusive line of shops round the block—an idea bubbling at the back of his brain. He didn't bother going back up to the office, got the car and went to the warehouse early to pick her up instead. Lorenzo was on the phone and waved his hand towards the stairs.

He could hear her voice. Given that Cara finished up early

afternoon, he knew she was on a call. He hovered outside the door so he wouldn't interrupt her.

'But this is my brother. Doesn't that count for something?'

Oh, it was a personal call. Alex stilled completely. He shouldn't listen. He'd done it before and suffered—losing the last of his childhood innocence as he'd realised his mother was having an affair. He didn't know who the lover she'd been talking to was—hadn't registered the extent of it, certainly hadn't dreamed there'd be that direct implication for him. Not then. But it had been a bitter enough pill. He'd been so angry with her—disrespecting her so much that Samuel had sent him to boarding school. The blindness of the man he'd thought was his father—whom he'd loved as his father—had made Alex even angrier.

So given what he knew about listening in to other people's conversations, he should walk down the hall and give Dani some privacy now. But his feet wouldn't move.

'But our mother is dead. How can she file the request when she's dead?'

He heard her sigh.

'But how can I find him if I can't get the paperwork from you?'

Silence while whoever it was talked some more.

'I'm in Auckland—what if I came into the office?'

Whoever it was, he was letting her down. Alex couldn't stop bending forward a fraction so he could see her through the gap in the hinge of the door. Her head was bent, her fringe hiding her eyes. From her slump he guessed the answer she'd just got was another negative.

'Is there any other way I might be able to find him?' She listened for a while. 'I've already put messages up on the Internet.' She was silent as she listened, and clearly not happy. 'OK. I understand. Thank you for your time.'

She put the phone down and buried her face in her hands, elbows thumping onto the desk.

Alex straightened and counted to five before walking on the spot for a few paces and then opening the door. 'Are you ready to leave?'

Her head snapped up. 'Alex. I didn't know you were here.' A flush mounted in her cheeks. 'I was using the phone but it was a local call.'

'It's fine to use the phone.' He was dying to ask more but she stood quickly and became busy pulling on her jacket. OK, he'd bide his time—but he'd find out what the deal was. She didn't suit the defeated look.

She said nothing until they were belted into his car, but then she launched a hit. 'I thought you said Cara was pregnant.'

Alex winced. Yeah, he should have seen this one coming. 'She is.'

'Not exactly due next month, though, is she?'

'No.' More like seven or so months. Cara had told them a couple of weeks ago, too effervescent to keep the news to herself any longer. She'd bounced off the walls when she'd blabbed it, while her husband had been all teasing protectiveness—warning that she wasn't to work too hard. Ironic when he was the CEO of one of the country's biggest accountancy firms and worked dog hours as bad as both Alex and Lorenzo.

'She's had terrible morning sickness.' Alex said, amazed at his inventiveness. Then he panicked, knowing the way women talked to each other. 'But don't mention it. She's very private. She doesn't want us to think she can't cope.'

'Oh.' Dani nodded. 'Of course. And is that why she works part-time hours at the moment?'

'Yes.' Lying was allowed when it was to help someone, right?

* * *

'You nearly ready?' Alex hollered.

Dani gave herself one last despairing glance in the mirror and fully regretted declining the use of the stylist.

Style—of the Carlisle standard. Could it be bought? Fashioned from the rawest of material? The dress was good, she knew it was good—it fitted perfectly. But the body beneath wasn't perfect, and there was no glitz or glam to dazzle the eyes and blind them to those imperfect bits.

She turned her back on her image and walked down the stairs to the lounge. He wasn't there. She took the few steps into the kitchen. He had his back to her. His perfectly fitted, perfectly pressed suit gleamed blacker than ink and oozed expense. He looked lean and long and definitely strong—could his shoulders be any broader? Then he turned around.

It took several moments before she could drag her gaze all the way up his body to his face. Even so his mouth was still hanging open, still another beat before he shut it. The surprise written all over him stung. Had he really expected her to walk in wearing some ill-fitting off-the-rack budget-chain number?

She was so glad she'd packed it. She'd laughed at her mother for making it. Argued she'd have been better off making her some more work shirts and skirts. Her mother had always altered her clothes for her—her breasts were too ample and her shoulders too narrow for store-bought to sit right. But she'd wanted to make her a dress—'to look beautiful' in. She'd despaired of Dani's jeans and tee habit. Just as Dani had despaired of her mother's 'must have a man' complex.

'Where did you get it?' He swallowed.

'My mother made it.' She cleared her throat. 'She was a seamstress.'

'A very good one.'

'Yes.' It was as beautifully made as his suit, which frankly she couldn't bear to look at a second longer. But the sting from his shock had gone now and left the heat of relief. She pushed her hair behind her ear. 'Should we get going?'

He walked over to her. 'I have something for you.' He reached into his pocket. 'To keep that bit out of your eyes.' He uncurled his fingers.

She had a quick peek and resolutely looked back up at him. 'I'm not wearing that.' And she wasn't going to look at it again. Her retinas were suffering enough already—bright spots danced the rumba before her.

'It's just a hairclip.'

It wasn't just a clip. It was a very grown-up piece of art. She might not have money but she wasn't stupid. Those weren't zirconias or even crystals. Only diamonds sparkled like that. It was an iris, wrought in a fine gold setting, some petals studded with diamonds, others decorated with yellow stones and a long slender gold stem. It was so, so pretty. Exactly the sort of totally feminine thing she secretly adored. How could he have known that? She couldn't deny she was thrilled. But even so, she couldn't possibly wear it. 'Where did you get it?'

He tilted his hand so it caught more light.

'I've never seen a clip like that.'

'It's a brooch—I got them to convert it.'

'Got who?'

'The jeweller.'

Oh, no. Her instinct was right—and no way could she accept something so expensive. 'Alex, I—'

He moved so close she could smell him—fresh and citrussy and so yummy she had to shut her mouth to stop herself drooling over him. His hands were firm on her head as he swept her hair back and pressed the clip into place.

He didn't move away once it was done. His hands dropped but he stayed.

She looked up at him. His eyes were a vivid green and a small smile tweaked his lips—as if he knew how much she liked it. She shook her head but he spoke first, not giving her the chance to say no.

'It looks better on you than it would on me.'

Alex marched five paces away from her—putting the stainless-steel bench between them. Breathing space—he needed it *now*. But he couldn't stop staring. He'd seen many black evening dresses in his time. He'd seen them long, short, high cut, low cut, backless, strapless, sleeveless, braless, sequined, sparkly, matte, smooth, velvet, silk, satin. He'd seen them twirl and he'd seen them creased. He'd helped slide zips both up and down. And he'd seen many of them slither to the floor.

But he had never, ever seen a black dress like hers. It fitted so perfectly. Utterly emphasising her petite, hourglass frame—cupping her full breasts, hugging her deliciously narrow waist and sweeping over those curving hips. Her short bob was sleek and glossy and there was that lock that slipped from behind her ear and curled on her cheekbone and he'd just had to deal with it—because if he didn't he'd spend the night tempted to swish it back with his teeth. His trawl of the jewellery stores had paid off. Now the clip sparkled, but not half as much as her eyes.

She was stunning.

'We should get going.' He didn't recognise his own voice. Apparently he had laryngitis now.

Ten minutes later Alex looked for the fiftieth time from the road to her, his head clear of all the confusion that had fogged it for this past week. His focus was sharp—on one thing: getting close to Dani. The urge to conquer was all-consuming. Driving every other thought beyond the mountains and into the sea. Right now, having her was all that mattered and damn the stupid complications.

It was amazing how someone so small could inspire such a big reaction in him. Although she wasn't that small—not where it counted.

'You look beautiful.' Such a useless cliché. And not nearly enough. But he was incapable of more.

'Not as beautiful as you,' she said.

She might think she was being flippant, but he knew she actually meant it. He'd seen the way she'd looked at him—the way her attention clung, the way her brown eyes darkened even more when he moved closer. And he was determined to move closer still. The frustration was immense. If it hadn't been for them getting caught on camera he could have had her already—couldn't he? Taken her on a date and ended up in bed. Surely she wouldn't have resisted?

But in his bones he knew she would have. The look she'd given him as she'd left the lift? Terrified. Turned on, yes, but terrified too. Fortunately her head had been away from the camera because he wouldn't have been crowned an online Don Juan if those in the blogosphere had seen her expression then. In his office she'd said it was nothing—a moment. Frankly he just didn't believe that. Sarcasm was her favourite form of defence—it had taken him only minutes to learn that. So he wanted a real-life replay of the lift kiss to prove his point—that the spark didn't get better than the one between them.

He steered the car with one hand, curled the other in a fist on his thigh. He wasn't going to drink tonight—that would only inflame the heat coursing through his body. He was on the edge of control as it was. It would need only the smallest provocation to tip him over the edge. Alex had never been on an edge quite like this before and he didn't like feeling so close to it now. And Dani was nothing but provocative.

'Where is this thing anyway?' She fidgeted—running her fingers over the edge of her dress. He really wanted her to stop because he was watching and all he wanted was for it to be *his* fingers feeling the transition from smooth silk to soft skin.

'Sky City.' The laryngitis was back.

She turned sharply towards him. 'I can't, Alex.'

Her voice was so panicked he nearly drove into the gutter.

'I can't go up in that lift.' Her huge eyes were even bigger and *so* dark.

Oh, dear, he should have thought of that. But damned if he could be bothered climbing however many million flights of stairs it was to get to the top of the tower that overlooked the city. He was just going to have to help her through the thirty-second ordeal. And just like that he had a plan. 'It'll be OK. I'll help you.' It would be his pleasure to.

She said nothing more but he felt her tension mounting as they drew closer to the brightly lit building and turned into its basement car park.

He could see her breasts rising too quickly as they waited but she walked in, head high. She stood with her back against the wall of the lift. He followed her but didn't turn to face the door, just stood bang in front of her—only an inch between them.

'I'm getting a sense of *déjà vu*.' He looked her over with deliberate boldness.

'Don't even think about it,' she croaked.

Oh, yes, he totally wanted to distract her that way again.

Press her against the wall and kiss her senseless so she wound herself round him again. Was that all it had been for her? A way of escaping her stress about riding in an elevator?

Her chest was still rising abnormally fast, but he saw her nipples had peaked now too. So he had her a little distracted.

'You can't stop me thinking, Dani.' Unfortunately he couldn't stop himself thinking, either—and he was thinking about it all the time.

She flicked a look up over his shoulders, lost colour as the door slid shut. He couldn't stop her thoughts, either, but maybe he could get her even more distracted—to think about something other than her fear.

He lifted a finger, traced the full curve of her lips. She hadn't plastered them in thick lipstick, but they did have a shine to them. Very pretty, very full, totally kissable. The colour returned to her cheeks in a sweep.

'I told you not…' Her feeble whisper died away as he stepped closer.

He ran his fingers up her cheekbone, turning his hand to brush the back of his fingers on her soft skin. She had a sweetheart-shaped face. Those big brown eyes dominated it. Her nose he'd barely noticed because of her drown-you-deep eyes and then there was the lush mouth beneath. But now, as he stood so close, he saw there were two freckles—one off to the left of the bridge of her nose, and one right near the tip. The tip of his finger circled them. He was going to have to kiss them.

Yeah, she was sweetheart pretty all right, with a body soft and curvy and built to contrast with his hard one. And when she opened her mouth it was all sarcasm and sass. The combination had him caught tighter than a fly in a spider's web—and he wanted her to suck him dry.

Wide-eyed, she gazed back at him, her breathing growing

choppier—but he liked to think it wasn't all about being shut up in a lift. Maybe she was reading his mind. If she was, then she knew she had far more to worry about than any stupid lift.

He heard the doors slide. They were there.

He took her hand in his, tightening his grip when she'd have pulled it away. 'Time to have a ball, Dani.'

CHAPTER SIX

DANI was so hot she could barely breathe. All the people she'd met tonight must think she was an idiot. She'd hardly been able to talk. It had been full on introduction after introduction, conversation and speculation and adoration—of him. But he hadn't left her side. Had turned to her when people asked questions, included her in the answering, not speaking for her but supporting her as she'd quietly replied.

He was doing it deliberately—touching her, looking at her like that—making it feel as if they were the only two in the room when in reality they were surrounded by hundreds. It was obvious everyone thought they were together. Not surprising given he was acting as if they were. And like a mythical beast it uncoiled between them, flexing the kind of strength no human had a hope of beating. It was the one thing that would reduce even the most sensitive, erudite, highly evolved person to the animal they really were—*lust*.

They moved together on the dance floor—his eyes glinted, teasing as he drew her closer then spun her away again. Oh, he would have all the fancy dance moves, wouldn't he?

'I need a drink,' Dani begged, needing a breather from him more than anything.

He chuckled as if he knew and led her by the hand towards the bar, letting her have her little respite.

'Alex.'

Dani turned at the unfamiliar voice, at the urgency with which it had spoken. But just as quick she looked at Alex because his hand suddenly crushed hers—his grip had gone boa-constrictor tight.

He'd frozen. His ready smile wiped. He didn't even say hello to the man who'd threaded his way to where they stood. He was about an inch shorter than Alex and dressed in a suit that Dani recognised as made to order. Flecks of grey peppered his dark hair, but despite his age he was still a good-looking man—a hint of charisma in the smooth face, his smile practised.

'I hoped you'd be here tonight.' Yes, the smile was definitely practised, because his eyes were too watchful, betraying a hint of uncertainty. 'I've tried calling you.'

Alex didn't even blink.

The man shifted, glanced at Dani and offered her a wider version of the smile before his attention flicked back to Alex. 'Aren't you going to introduce me?'

The silence stretched. The awkwardness excruciating. What was the problem here? Didn't Alex want to introduce her? But instinctively she knew it was this man that he had the problem with, not her. And it was some problem—she'd never have guessed a master of people skills like Alex could be so impolite.

'Dani, this is Patrick. Patrick, this is Dani.' He finally spoke. No qualifiers, no descriptors, no other info. Just names. Totally different from how he'd spoken with any of the others they'd mingled with tonight. His face had gone totally mask-like. 'I didn't realise you were in New Zealand.'

'I thought it would be a good idea. I take it you've had the results back.'

'Yes.' Alex's mouth barely moved as he replied, his eyes like stones.

Dani felt goose bumps rise over every inch of her skin. Alex's voice was blowing a chill direct from Antarctica.

The two men stared at each other. Alex stood ramrod straight and still, unrelenting in his cold scrutiny.

'It would be good to talk.' Patrick shifted his feet, his tongue touching the corner of his lip.

Was that the faintest touch of a plea in his comment? Dani almost felt afraid—the undercurrents swirling between the men seemed dark and downright dangerous. *Alex* seemed dangerous. The aggression she could feel mounting in him was raw. And this silence was too horribly long.

'Not now.' Alex shattered it. Brutally dismissive. Unbelievably cold. Then he turned, practically dragging Dani away with him.

Dani swallowed and half skipped to keep up. Stunned by this facet of Alex she hadn't known existed. He went straight to the bar, ordered her a wine and himself a neat whisky. He knocked it back in one swallow. It was the first drop of alcohol he'd had all night. Dani sipped her wine slowly, wondering if he was going to have another, wondering what it was about the Patrick man that had him feeling so lethal. But he turned, looked her over, his eyes nothing but fire now.

'Dance with me.'

She couldn't refuse, her heart thudding as she felt the barely leashed emotion in him. He held her close—much closer than when they'd danced before. The music was loud, the tempo fast, but all the energy zinged from him— electrifying her nerves. And then she felt the change within him, from anger, to passion—but no less intense. He pulled her closer still, his hands firm on her body—moulding her to him. The way he moved was incredible, intoxicating, dizzying—indeed she stumbled.

He took her by the elbow and led her to a secluded table on the far side of the dance floor. He poured her a glass of water from the carafe on the table.

Dani took a sip of the cool liquid and asked before she lost the nerve. 'Who's Patrick?'

His eyes were dark, unreadable in the flashing lights from the dance floor. 'No one.'

She had another sip of water, unsurprised by his answer. It wasn't any of her business anyway. He pulled his chair closer, facing her rather than out to the floor. And then his hands disappeared.

'What are you doing?' She could hardly move her mouth enough to ask.

'Nothing.' Beneath the table his fingers were lightly caressing her knee—rubbing over the silk hem of her dress and onto her skin.

Nothing? Nothing like the lift?

His fingers moved higher.

'I'd have thought a high-society fundraising dinner wouldn't be the place for public displays of lust,' she choked. 'Aren't you too well bred for that?'

'Who said I was well bred?' His hand slid higher up her thigh, the touch suddenly far more insistent.

Dani gulped. 'I thought you were staying away.'

'Was I?'

'Stop it.'

Make me. He didn't say it. He didn't need to. He was so used to getting his way, wasn't he? He understood the power of his charm. The way people had fawned over him tonight proved it. He thought he could get away with anything.

And maybe he could.

But Dani was suddenly filled with the urge to better him—just the once. The thrill of the challenge was irresistible, and what better way to drive away the shadows in his eyes from his frosty encounter with Patrick?

'All right.' She turned towards him. 'If this is what you want.'

She lifted her hand to his face, ran her hand down his smooth jaw. Leaned closer and breathed in. She loved the light, crisp scent of his aftershave. She dropped her hand to his chest, feeling the beat of his heart and its acceleration, the heat of his skin burning through the shirt. Sizzling—that was Alex.

She moved her hand again, placed it lower—far higher up his thigh than his fingers had ventured up hers. She twisted her wrist, spreading her fingers, stroking his already rigid length, encircling it and then squeezing.

She was unable to stop her smile as he stopped breathing. His discomfort registered even more on his face. His mouth snapped shut, jaw went militarily square. She saw the ripple in his muscles as he struggled for control.

She leaned closer, her mouth a millimetre from his skin, and teased him some more. 'Dare you to walk across the dance floor now.'

His breath hissed out between his teeth as he jerked, flinging far back into his seat and out of her reach. No, he wasn't really into public displays at all, was he?

Triumphant, she met his eyes, her smile widening with the thrill of the dangerous line she was treading.

But then he moved. His grip on her upper arm was hard and he stood so fast that she stumbled as he hauled her up beside him. His other hand went around her waist, clamping her so she was just in front of him. He pressed his hot, hard body against her back. Insistent, he pushed her forward.

She walked. She had no choice. Right across the dance floor.

But he didn't release her once they were clear; instead he guided her out of the room completely, down a corridor, and left, down another corridor.

Halfway along that he swiftly turned her, his arms powerful as he pulled her close. He pressed her against him, one hand slid beneath the hem of her dress. Her knees sagged at the touch and he pushed her until her back hit the wall. But he kept pushing until his body was sealed hard to the length of hers. Save a scrap of satin, a whisper of silk and his strained trousers, they were as intimate as two people could physically be.

Her gasp rasped in her ears and her most feminine muscles clenched instinctively, the hungry ache down low unbearable.

'Don't play with me and think you can win.' His words dropped into her ear like sparks of wildfire—igniting frustration, temptation and anger. He felt so good against her. So incredibly good. She gazed at him, anticipation smothering any chance of thought.

'My turn to dare,' he taunted.

Her awareness surged to new heights, her body supersensitive.

'Kiss me.' He'd loosened his hold yet she couldn't escape, couldn't make herself push away the heat. Instead she wanted him closer again.

Pleasure and satisfaction—his promise of both beckoned her. His fingers stroked her thigh, inching higher, then higher, delicately tracing across her soft skin and sending ripples of sensation out to the rest of her body—especially those secret parts.

'Kiss me.' He flexed—closer—a minuscule movement with maximum impact.

Her lashes drooped as she studied him up close, no longer

conscious of anything else but him. He tilted his chin at her, just the way she had at him in the lift that day, and his lips twisted into that irresistible smile.

And she couldn't resist him. Not when he looked so good, smelt so good, felt so good. Her lips parted, her body going on instinct now, her brain defunct. All she could see was his mouth—almost parted, waiting—and the desire in his eyes. All she could hear was the thunder of her heart as it sent hot blood racing through her body.

As her head lifted, her lashes dropped, blocking everything so she could focus only on the sensation of his mouth against hers. Even so just the briefest touch overwhelmed her; she shivered. His whole body tensed. He lifted his hand from her back, tangling his fingers in her hair, keeping her close to him so she wouldn't break the contact of their lips. Not that she could. Not now, no. She threaded both her hands through his hair too, clinging, so eager for more than a taste of him. She moved her lips over his. He had full lips, firm and yet soft. She touched them with her tongue, tasting, then pushing closer, exploring the heat of his mouth. More. And then more still.

He let her dominate for a moment, but then rewarded her hungry searching with a deep thrust of his own. Involuntary spasms racked her as he held her close and plundered. Her fingers tightened in his hair as she tumbled headlong into his stormy passion.

The hand between her legs coasted higher, skimming across the satin of her knickers, making her squirm, making her wish she could arch against him freely. His hand spread wide against the back of her head, holding her even more firmly to him. She felt his groan vibrate through his whole body as he stroked her intimately. His fingers gently moved back and forth as he savoured the damp evidence of her desire for him—desire hurtling her to abandonment.

She opened deeper for him, the kiss almost savage now as the full power of their physical attraction was unleashed. She pressed against his chest, trying to please her painfully taut nipples with contact against his hard heat.

The high-pitched laughter and the tinging of glass on glass screeched over the roar in her ears. Her eyes snapped open, shattering the moment. Suddenly she was aware of where they were.

'Stop, Alex,' she panted against his mouth. She could see the sheen on his skin and fiercely suppressed the urge to lick the salty flavour of him.

His breath gusted across her face as he pulled back.

'Not here.' As close to a plea as she'd ever uttered. They were in a public space. A minute or two more of that kind of kissing and she was going to be coming loud and wild only a thin wall away from Auckland's most rich and famous. Her heart pounded so hard she thought it must be about to blow apart in her body. The physical need burned through to her bones. She tore her gaze from his, made herself look along the corridor— Oh, hell, someone had just walked past. They'd only have to turn their head to see them. Alex's broad body partially protected her privacy, but even so.

Lust had made her forget everything—who she was, where she was, and what she was supposed to be doing. A different kind of heat engulfed her.

Humiliation.

Dani refused to let desire turn her into such a mindless *slave*.

'Let's go.' Temptation personified murmured into her ear.

If she went with him this minute they'd end up in the back seat of his car, or in the loo on the way, or a cleaning cupboard, or down an alley, or something equally tacky but convenient. So she had to claw back her self-control fast because having sex with Alex wouldn't just be reckless, it would be dangerous. The feelings he aroused in her were too strong. She couldn't let herself drown in them. Her response wasn't just physical, it would be over-emotional too. All Alex was up for was a little playtime—she needed time out to get a grip first. 'Aren't you supposed to draw some prize or something?'

'Lorenzo can do it.'

'You can't let them down.' She pushed him away. He moved and she smoothed down the front of her dress in a quick gesture.

'It's your turn to dare,' he said too coolly, too confidently.

She shook her head. 'I'm all out of challenges.'

He chuckled. 'I don't believe that.' He stepped closer again. 'Maybe you just need some provocation.' He leant forward and kissed her again, his mouth seeking, demanding. She bit back the moan. He wasn't touching her anywhere else but she ached to ride him, to rock her hips back and forth and take him inside her. If they were alone she would do just that. Shed her clothes and his and have all of him hard and fast and right *now*.

She tore free of his kiss and gulped in air. But no matter how many breaths she took she still felt dizzy. She stared at him, shocked at the need still rampaging through her defences. So easily he had won this from her. So much for staying away—so much for either of them having self-control.

'What do you think about a truce?' She was panting too much for the question to come out as tart as she'd have liked.

He lifted his hand and ran the tip of his finger over her lips. She gasped again.

'We can delay a little longer if you like. But this is inevitable.'

She wanted to shake her head but it felt heavy and she

couldn't move it. Passion shone in his eyes, pleasure and satisfaction broadened his smile.

'We're flatmates,' she finally managed. 'We can be friends but we can't…' She trailed off as he laughed.

'Honey, we can't be friends. Not 'til we've burned this out.' He nudged her chin with his thumb. 'After that we can—I get on well with all my ex-lovers.'

Oh. Was that so? 'Regular Lothario, aren't you?' Dani drawled, sarcasm dripping.

'Well, you have your *joy* boys—right?' His smile had sharp edges. 'Nothing wrong with liking sex, Dani. It's natural.'

Slack jawed, she could no longer cope with his subtle-as-a-brick sensuality. Because the worst thing about it was that it made her body burn hotter. 'I need to freshen up.'

'Coward.'

How long was it possible to live with an Empire-State-Building-size erection? Alex wondered whether there was an entry in the Guinness Book of Records and knew with certainty that if there was, he was going to beat it.

'You're taking her home?'

'To her separate little bedroom, yes.'

Lorenzo laughed. 'That won't last long.'

Alex leant his shoulder against the wall. From here he could see when she exited the bathroom. 'It's complicated.'

'Yeah. The whole Internet movie, invent her a job, move her into your home kind of complicated.'

Alex shook his head. Lorenzo didn't know the half of it. He didn't know the whole I-just-found-out-who-my-father-really-is nightmare yet. And it was a nightmare. Alex swept a quick glance around the room, couldn't see the bastard. How dared Patrick just appear like that—what was he trying to do? What did he want? Well, whatever it was, he wasn't getting it.

That was really what was eating Alex alive, not some five-foot-nothing sexy piece of a woman. He sighed as the thought of Dani made his whole body ache with need. 'It was your dumb idea to move her in to my place.'

'Thought it might be convenient.' Lorenzo chuckled.

Alex shot him a filthy look and drained the last of his juice. OK, so she was eating him up too. But he could deal with lust, couldn't he? Wasn't he Alex Carlisle? Didn't he have a phone full of names and numbers of wannabe dates? If he wanted sex he could get it, no problem.

But he'd happily fling the thing in the harbour. Normally he did a few dates, a few laughs, never anything complicated and certainly not committed—a two-months sort of man, that was him. Women were for fun, nothing more—he was never having anything more. But now he wanted sex with only one woman. The scent of her incited an untapped depth of hunger in him. He didn't know how he was going to assuage it. There were so many options, so many fantasies swirling in his head all the damn time.

So much of it was the game, wasn't it? The hunt, the chase, the challenge she threw at him. Since when had he had to work for it like this—or to wait? Usually he didn't bother if someone was giving him the hard-to-get routine. He wasn't that desperate. But Dani was different. She didn't want a 'relationship'. Fantastic. But her determined denial of a fun fling bit him hard. This time the game was everything. Oh, yeah, he was getting off on every minute of it and doing everything he could to aggravate a response from her.

He straightened as he saw her appear. If he were to judge by the look on her face he wasn't getting any further with her tonight, but, judging by the tension in her body, he figured he had another shot. And he was damn well taking it.

Dani waited with him for the lift and focused on her breathing—the last of her Alex-induced heat doused by the fear of the few seconds to come. So stupid to be like this. But every time she got into a small space her stomach knotted and all the oxygen vanished. Every time she remembered the darkness, and the silence—the terrifying silence that had been shattered by that vicious thud.

Alex pulled her into the hideous rectangle. 'Look at me.' He pointed to his eyes. 'Look right here.'

She glared at him. Cross with his patronising attitude. 'Look, I'm not some mad cow and you're not some animal whisperer with a mesmerising gaze.'

'Dani.' He took her upper arms in his broad hands and gently shook her. 'You're totally a mad cow.'

'Yeah.' She barely registered her pathetic reply because he did have magical green eyes. They were twinkling right now and imparting some kind of secret message.

She stumbled as he let her go with an ironic murmur. 'Look at that—we're on the ground already.'

As they walked to his car the dark quiet night seemed to swallow them. The thick silence kept them company all the drive home.

She climbed the stairs. Her pulse stepping up a notch, and then another, then more in rapid succession until she was filled with more adrenalin than when she'd been frozen with fear in the cupboard that day.

He pressed buttons for the alarm system. She heard the keys land on the wood of the table and walked even faster, keen to get to her room, *alone*. He caught her arm, his hand sliding to her wrist. She stopped. He had to feel that galloping rhythm in her veins. She heard him step closer and fought to keep the feeling of fear. That would give her strength.

He kissed the nape of her neck, kept near enough for her to feel his breath warm her skin. 'When were you last serviced, sweetheart?' The smile was soft in his voice. 'Seems to me you're in need of a tune-up.'

Dani couldn't breathe, let alone answer. All the old fear dissolved—*she* was dissolving.

His laugh was low and sexy. 'You said about your men, Dani, but it's all a tale.'

'What makes you think that?'

'Because when it comes down to the moment, you hesitate.' He turned her to face him. 'You're not off having one-night stands all over the place or maintaining an assortment of lovers. You go so far, and, honestly, it's not even that far. Then you stop.'

All talk and no action, huh? OK, so there might be some truth in that. Not that she'd admit to it.

'I'm even starting to wonder if you're a virgin,' he teased.

She choked. OK, so she didn't have anywhere near the kind of experience she'd implied, but she wasn't that. She looked at the third button down on his shirt and assumed a bored tone. 'Maybe I'm just not that into you.'

'Oh, but you are.' He bent so it wasn't his buttons she saw but his smile—the one that lit up his whole face. 'Want me to prove it to you?'

His pursuit was in earnest now. She could see the determination, the seriousness in his eyes, feel it in every deliberate touch. He'd said that they were inevitable. And if she were honest she'd have to agree. So why was she bothering with the fight? Why not give in?

Because she didn't want to be his latest prize. Sure, he was compelling, charming. But he was also competitive, driven to win. She suspected he could be ruthless about that. He'd been born to succeed and obviously thrived on it. And right now *she* was the challenge—but that was all she was. She felt like a bug in the path of a steamroller. And there was that innate part of her that always fought—not to be the statistic, not to do the expected, never to give up or give in.

But most of all she didn't want to open herself up. Because she had the feeling that Alex would take more than she intended to give. She liked to be in control of her emotions—but she couldn't see herself keeping that control in his arms. Not when he made her feel like some mindless nympho with just one kiss and a pet or two. So, even in the face of the impossible, she made her stand.

'Actually I'll pass, Alex.' She walked to the relative safety of the doorway. Then she went for the flick-off. 'You know, you're right, it has been a while. I found my servicemen to be a little lacking. But, you know, a girl can do so much better for herself.' She fluttered her fingers up past her breast, to her mouth, and watched his slightly stunned expression widen even more. 'Infinitely more reliable. Satisfying.' She ran the tip of her index finger across her lower lip, let her tongue touch it briefly. 'I can take care of my needs myself. I don't need anyone else.'

CHAPTER SEVEN

HEAVY-HEADED and grumpy, Dani dragged herself from bed more frustrated than a sex addict trapped in solitary for three years. Because that was exactly what she was, wasn't it? Some kind of sad addict—craving for his touch, his kiss. It was just because it had been ages, right? That was why her hips were so keen to wriggle now. But her hips had never wanted to wriggle as bad as this.

She imprisoned them in her most conservative black skirt and topped it with a pale blue blouse. Thick black opaque tights helped keep her legs warm and hidden and her wedge-heeled shoes gave her some help in the height department—stilettos weren't something her ex-tomboy self could walk in.

She brushed her hair, took care applying her usual light layer of make-up. Armour. She needed conservative today.

She stared at the finished result in the mirror and sighed. The frustration was evident on her face—her increased pallor, the shadows under her eyes. Hell, she was letting him mess with her looks. Not good. Was she becoming as much of a victim as her mother? Letting a man upset the life she was trying so hard to get on track?

Maybe, she should just have sex with him and be done with it. She wanted to—*how* she wanted to. And wasn't she overanalysing the whole thing? Wasn't she overstating the effect he had on her? Wasn't it just because she hadn't had sex in eons? Couldn't he be exactly the kind of fling she'd said she did—routine 'maintenance'. No emotion. No complication. Just fun—it was just sex, after all. And once done, it was done. Why, then they could be *friends*.

That was how he did it, right? He'd said it was *just sex, just fun*. Surely if she went in eyes wide-open, she wouldn't make the mistake of making more of it. Surely with this awareness, she could stay in control?

She walked down the stairs into the kitchen. Got halfway to the pantry before she finally looked at him and stopped—impaled by his intense stare. Long moments disappeared into a vortex while he somehow looked over every inch of her outfit yet held her eyes captive with his.

Her nipples tightened; so did the muscles in her womb. It wasn't going away. And it was only getting worse.

Owl-like, she closed her eyes and moved her head down, opening her eyes again, she saw her shirt and skirt. She hadn't realised it, but it was the exact outfit she'd been wearing that day in the lift. OK, maybe she had realised but had been in denial. The look in his eyes had told her he remembered too.

'Have a good night?' he asked way too intensely. 'Enjoy playing by yourself in that big bed?'

Oh, yeah, her hollow words came back to haunt her. What a joke that had been. She'd shifted round restlessly the whole night. She wanted only one thing—his body filling hers. She frowned.

He leaned back against the bench and ran his hand up his chest to his heart, drawing *her* attention to *his* fine physique displayed in his crisp white shirt. 'Don't ruin my fantasy now.' He tilted his head, studied her with half-closed eyes and a smile born of wickedness. 'You know I'd love to watch.'

'Pervert.' But she felt the blush covering her skin. Even worse a ripple of excitement stirred in her belly. She couldn't really *want* like this, could she?

She moved. The pantry. Cereal. Breakfast. Then work. But her blood pounded, deafening her. She'd had enough of this starvation. She went into the small room and tried to find some food—what had happened to his host act? Why hadn't he made her breakfast?

She heard a sound, glanced behind her, his body filled the frame of the doorway into this tiny space.

Ragged-breathed, butter-fingered, trembling—she couldn't even pour the cereal.

'Is it the small space? That's what's upsetting you so much?'

So he'd noticed—hard not to when she'd dropped the box of crunchy clusters twice already.

Her mouth was dry. The swallow hurt. 'No.'

'Then why are you so on edge?'

She spun on her toes to face him, now he stood a mere whisper away. 'You know why.'

He held her gaze as he had only minutes before. The green of his eyes disappeared in the darkness as his pupils swelled.

She was fascinated. And suddenly she was decided. She was determined—in control. 'If we do this,' she said firmly, 'then you're with no one else while I'm with you.'

His eyes flashed fire. 'Do you really think it necessary to make that clear?'

'You kiss complete strangers in elevators. Of course it's necessary.'

'Yeah, well, you admit to spreading your legs like margarine for a whole *variety* of men. So no other lovers for you, either.'

She adopted a faux crushed look, gave an equally faux sigh. 'It'll be hard. But I guess I can find the discipline somehow.'

He lifted his hand and waved his palm at her. 'I can help you with discipline if you want, honey.'

Her jaw dropped. 'Don't you dare.'

His low laughter sent waves of want pulsing from her belly outwards.

'It's *my* turn to dare.' She wrested back the lead.

He sobered instantly. 'What do you want me to do?'

Her answer was short. Explicit. And very, very naughty.

'Now?' He was already moving.

'Yes.'

'Here?'

'Just hurry up.' She reached for him with both hands, mouth open.

Ravenous.

He met her more than halfway. The pressure of his lips bruised but still it wasn't close enough. She mewled into his mouth and pushed her whole body closer. And what had begun that day in the lift surged forward, continuing at breakneck speed towards the only possible conclusion. She rubbed against him, so eager to explore him, to have his thighs between hers, to have his hands there too, his mouth and most of all his rock-hard penis. Everything, all at once. Right now.

He moved, kissing her cheek, her neck, down to her chest, pulling the shirt aside so he could access skin. She fumbled with buttons, cursing when they wouldn't undo as fast as she needed them to. She grabbed his hair and yanked, bringing his mouth back to hers. She gasped for air when she could and dived straight back into the heat of his kisses, the need burning her up. She arched against him, her hips writhing round and round in a mad rhythm.

Now. She wanted him there now.

He ripped his lips from hers. Swore. 'I don't want to stop.'

'Hell, no, *don't*.' Feverish, she raked her hands down his back, urging him closer.

'Contraception,' he cursed. 'I don't want to screw up this situation even more.'

'I'm covered.' She nipped his mouth angrily. 'I'm never having an unplanned pregnancy. Get on with it.'

Still he paused. 'I've never want—'

'Me, either.'

Passion spiralled higher. Never had she wanted a man to be inside her the way she wanted him. She worked fast, desperate to get her hands on his bare skin. Feral, crazed. Fabric tore and buttons burst.

Her fingers curled into his hard muscles, not just testing their strength, but provoking a forceful response with her sharp little nails. She wanted him—his body, his strength, his absolute attention.

Now.

Alex had never had such animal sex, ever. Usually he was courteous, making sure his partner was well satisfied before allowing his own release. It was frivolous, frisky, carefree. This was anything but. This felt like a battle to the death. He seized her round the waist as he had that day, pleasure rippling through his muscles as they exerted, lifting her up and pinning her back against the wall. Now he could press against her. Now he could have her.

She was still fighting like a wildcat—wanting him with an aggression that matched his. Tearing his shirt free of his trousers, she pulled at the buttons. Busy fighting for what she wanted while he was fighting to get what he wanted—her naked.

It was a mess. She was wearing tights and neither of them

could get them off her. In the end he got them as far down as her calves and then stepped over the stretchy Lycra so she could loop her legs around his waist. Her skirt was hitched up, her torn blouse hanging half open. He spared a half-second to suck a nipple into his mouth, bra and all. Her gasp felled him. He simply shredded her knickers. Oh, she was wet, and smelled so good and moved even better against the fingers he used to test her—clamping on them, promising insane pleasure.

Ready. So ready.

He moved. Suddenly, finally, thrust into her.

His heart seized.

The world fell away as he looked into her eyes, unable to move, unable to think, unable to believe how good he felt. How good *she* felt.

She too was frozen, her lips parted. In jagged bursts she released the breath she'd been holding. The moans that came with it were the sound of pure bliss.

It surged into him. Like a burst dam, emotion flooded him. Her fingers curled into his hair at the same moment. Wide eyed, shaking, she put her lips to his. Kissing him—the kind of soul-searing kiss that would have had him on his knees if he weren't suddenly imbued with the ability to handle super-human sensations. Sensations so raw he thought he'd die silently screaming with the pleasure.

At last their movements matched. They worked together, locking into the dance so deeply now. She met his hard thrusts with forceful ones of her own. Taking him further, her legs curled tighter around him. Her mouth was open, lips full and swollen as she panted, and then moaned with delight. Her sounds matched the rhythm of their bucking hips. He too was grunting in time with each pound, half crazed with the way she

made his body sing. Trying harder and harder to get closer—
to her, and to the blinding peak that was just out of reach.

He saw her bite down on her lips, her face screw tighter in
agony as ecstasy approached. She was flushed with pleasure
and that curling lock of hair flopped on the side of her face.

She was beautiful. Born for this. As was he. Her neck
arched as she threw her head back and he couldn't resist the
vulnerability of the soft skin.

Her scream sliced through his skin and bone, piercing right
into his marrow. And instinct took over, driving his body.
Surging harder, faster, seeing her ride the whole of the crest
before he lost it entirely. A guttural shout ripped from him—
hurting his throat, echoing relentlessly in the small room.

He kept his eyes closed. He felt the trickles down his face,
his back. How the hell had they got so sweaty in what had surely
been only a few minutes? He didn't think he'd ever catch his
breath. With one hand he gripped the edge of the shelf behind
her, trying to keep control, keep his mind conscious as the
blackness threatened to trap him completely. The overwhelming feeling, that post-orgasmic relief, had him trembling.

Trembling?

Intense didn't cover it. His lungs burned as he strove to get
more air in. At last he looked down at her. She looked shocked
and she couldn't wipe her expression in time to hide it from
him. But as he watched she shut it down; he saw the defensiveness veil her from him. All it did was make his body stir—
made him want to hold her close and do all kinds of things with
his hands and mouth. Because then she couldn't hide from
him—not when it was like this between them. And what she
hadn't been able to hide just then had satisfied him even more.

Out of control. She'd been as out of control as him.

Thank goodness for that.

* * *

Dani summoned her last crumb of energy and pushed him away. She stumbled in the attempt to untangle her legs from his and he hopped free, pulling up his boxers and trousers, wiping the sweat from his brow with a broad palm.

Dani's limbs shook. She needed to get out of here. Not because she was stuck in a small space, hell, she hadn't known where she was for the last few minutes—couldn't have cared less. But she was in a far more scary zone now. All that mattered was getting away from him—quickly, so she could pull herself together again. Else she was going to launch herself back into his arms and beg for more—beg for everything.

Sex was sex? Fun? Meaningless?

That hadn't been either.

That had been the most intense experience of her life. So wild. So wonderful. So scarily insane.

He grabbed her by the wrist as she made it to the doorway. 'We should talk, Dani.'

Um. Why? She didn't want a post-mortem on that moment. She wanted to wrap it up in tissue and put it pride of place in her memory chest.

'Not necessary.' She aimed for casual, struggled to walk in a dignified way given the remnants of her knickers and tights were down round her ankles and her shoes were still on. 'I have a job to get to,' she said shakily. 'So do you.' She yanked off one shoe and freed her foot from the tights.

'Work can wait.'

'I'm not walking in an hour late because I slept with the boss.' Actually she really ought to forget it. Go to a hypnotist and have the memory erased or something.

'I'm not your boss.'

'Semantics.' She raced to her room. 'I'll be ten minutes.'

She took twenty and that was still nowhere near long enough for her to recover. She was going to need a few centuries for that. Wow oh wow oh wow.

Who ever knew it could be like that? No wonder the man was so popular—and so confident.

He was ready and waiting downstairs, hair still drying from its obvious dunking in the shower. She looked away, heat flooding her. She didn't want to think about him naked in the shower.

'Dani—'

'Let's not, Alex,' she almost pleaded as she clipped down the stairs to the garage. 'You were right, it was inevitable. But we've done it now.'

'You think that's done?' He laughed. 'You've got to be kidding.'

Not at all. Not doing it again would be the most sensible thing by *far*. She was too inexperienced to play with a champ like him. 'Can we get going? It's only my second day on the job.'

He slammed the door and fired the engine. 'We're not done.'

'I'm not going to argue with you, Alex.'

'Good, because I'm right and you know it.'

She reached forward and turned the volume of the radio up and made a point of staring out of the side window.

Stupid, so completely stupid.

She'd known it, hadn't she? Her instincts had been bang on. Now her body was screaming chaos—wanting to cling but wanting to run just as much. Getting close to him was like volunteering to abseil into a live volcano—an adrenalin rush like no other, but with a high chance of incineration.

'Why are you in New Zealand, Dani? Are you looking for someone—your brother?'

Dani whipped round to look at him—how did he know that?

'I heard you on the phone last night,' he said bluntly.

The stitches holding the hurt in her heart ripped. That was her most private business, her greatest treasure, and she didn't want anyone—not even him—invading the preciousness of it. 'You shouldn't eavesdrop on private conversations.'

'I might be able to help.'

How? Did he have access to all those secret files? She couldn't breathe. Most certainly couldn't speak. Just stared back out of the window.

'Look, you don't have to tell me if you don't want to,' he said softly, 'but I know a really good private investigator.'

'What do you need a PI for?' she asked, surprised.

'Every family has its secrets, Dani.' His smile twisted.

'But not every family uses a PI to find them out.'

He went quiet as he turned into the car park in the front of Lorenzo's warehouse. She knew he was waiting but she'd never told a soul about Eli. He wasn't her secret, he was her mother's.

Finally he shrugged and switched off the engine. 'The offer is there.'

'I'll think about it,' she lied out of politeness. She wasn't sharing that with him—way too personal. 'Thanks,' she added as an afterthought.

He'd got out too, walked round to her side of the car, suddenly looking fiery. 'Do you have to wear those shirts?'

'What's wrong with my shirts?' They were beautifully fitted, hand-stitched in parts, and conservative. 'They're not too tight.' Not like some of the numbers she'd seen around his office.

'They *hint*.'

Hint? She frowned at a small noise. 'Are you grinding your teeth?'

'Now I know what's underneath…'

She looked at him as his voice trailed off, her gaze colliding with his. Longing tumbled over her and her legs went new-foal wobbly—she was feeling desperate for him again already? 'I'll dig out my caftan later.'

'Don't bother, I'll still see your curves.'

He claimed her hand with a 'don't even try to stop me' grip. So she didn't try, because the need in her body for some kind of touch was too strong.

'What are you doing?' And why did she have to be so breathless around him?

'Proving a point.'

But the last word never made it out because he pressed his lips to hers, his body pushing her back against the car, his hands sweeping over her. Dani's body both melted and went bowstring taut. So much for sex snapping the tension.

Alex lifted his head and smiled. She was flushed, soft in his arms and unbearably tempting. 'You'd better go in, sweetheart. You don't want to be late, do you?'

He laughed as she gave him a glare. Then he got back in his car and gunned it.

Sweet, mindless sex. Hours and hours of hard, physical, frisky distraction. That was what he needed and all he wanted. It was the one thing guaranteed to take his mind off his nightmarish family crisis. Images from last night flashed in his head—the shock he'd felt when he'd seen him: Patrick. He'd stared at him, searching for the familiar in his features. Hating himself for not having seen it before. Hating the man more for the years of lies.

Alex had worked and worked and worked for years—and for what? He had no right to the name, his mother had had no right to raise him thinking he did. No right to instil in him the sense of *duty* that had meant he'd never considered any other option—that his life had become the business.

He couldn't believe the extent of the deceit. Couldn't bear to think of the betrayal. It made him glad Samuel was dead—glad he'd never know the truth. Because it really sucked.

So Alex deserved some fun, didn't he? On tap in his own house. He wasn't going to let any stupid regrets take hold of Dani. He knew she was full of it—there weren't any joy boys. But he'd been blowing the hot stuff too—wasn't the total playboy he'd let her believe. Sure, he'd had a rampant phase for a few years there, but he'd matured. Only the occasional date had made it to first base, let alone third, recently, hardly any home runs. OK, he'd got bored.

But he wasn't bored now.

He'd help her with her search if she'd let him. He wanted her to get the answers she needed—he knew all too well how horrible it was not to have those answers. And while she might not want a relationship she was a touch romantic—with her pretty candles and lacy underwear—so he'd do some romancing. Because he wasn't letting her deny them the physical fling that he was sure would make them both feel fantastic, and let him forget everything else. Even if only for a while.

Cara was at her desk, her smile sly. Dani glanced out of her window—yeah, it overlooked the car park. OK, so that was embarrassing. Thank goodness Cara was too well bred to comment on anything so personal. There was a part of Dani that would have loved to share her anxiety and excitement—to have a good girly chat about it as she would have done with her mother or her old schoolmates. But she'd lost touch with those friends when her mother was so sick and her father had made it so much worse. Now her mother had gone and Dani didn't know Cara anywhere near well enough to confide.

Instead she got on with her work—sneaking time to post a

question on one of the adoption boards. She'd left messages on a reunion site for him but had no reply. What could she do next given she was unable to request his full file from the authorities?

And after Cara left in the early afternoon, Dani went back online. She wasn't into the whole online social networking thing. Even less so since she'd starred in a downloadable clip of her own. But right now she was a glutton for punishment. She typed in his name. And hers. Found the elevator kiss clip. Winced at the number of hits it had received and blushed beet red when she read some of the comments. People needed to get their own lives. She quickly logged back into the message board, hoping someone might have an answer for her. There was only one.

If he hasn't replied to the ads, there's not much else you can do without professional help. Hire a PI.

CHAPTER EIGHT

'ABOUT this morning.' Dani finally broached the subject.

'Yes?'

Dani glanced sideways at Alex, a touch apprehensive. He looked uncharacteristically stern, had been quiet on the drive home. 'I'm not sure we should repeat it.'

'Dani, be honest.' He served up something from the slow cooker his housekeeper had filled while they were at work. 'It was mind-blowing and you want to do it again as much as I do.'

'I don't want to screw up this situation even more.' She quoted his words back at him.

'Sleeping together isn't going to do that.' He reached for another plate and ladled food onto that too. 'You've made it clear you don't want a relationship. Well, neither do I. This is just sex. Just fun. Just for now.'

Bed buddies? That was all he wanted, wasn't it? The scenario she'd used to tease him with was the exact one he wanted from her—nothing more. While she'd known that, hearing him say it aloud made her heart beat horribly—skipping beats here and there.

He put the plate down, and the spoon, moved around the bench—and all the while didn't take his eyes off her.

'You don't want to eat?' Her pulse hammered in her ears.

'Not food.'

He was going to prove a point again, wasn't he? 'Alex—'

He leant close, touching her only with his lips. It was all he needed to do. Her lashes lowered as she felt the sensations wash over her. He was right—*mind-blowing*. She stepped forward, melted into his arms. Without breaking the kiss he lifted her, carried her up the stairs. And she was happy to let him carry her wherever so long as he kept on kissing her like that. The desire to be with him dominated everything.

He set her on her feet in his bedroom. 'Sweetheart.' He smiled as he set about stripping her, muttering more beneath his breath as her body was exposed to him. She was as keen to see him—grappled with the buttons on his shirt until he growled and got rid of it himself. When they were finally naked they stared at each other. His smile faded as he raked her body with his hot gaze. She shivered as she took in his beauty—the sculpted shoulders, defined muscles, the fine scattering of hair on his chest that arrowed down below his belly button, drawing her attention to his straining erection— his physique was sheer perfection and deep inside her a primal readying was occurring. She wanted him absolutely.

Their eyes met. His were fiery. Dani instinctively dampened her lips with her tongue and saw him tense even more. It was going to be explosive again. Good.

And with a suddenness that stole her breath he moved, tumbling her back onto the bed, lunging after her. As his body collided with hers there was instant friction, instant heat. He was so strong. She kissed him hungrily, those last little doubts in her head toppling like sandcastles in the tide. Sure it could be simple. It could just be sex.

His kiss was hot, his body strong. His lips and tongue probed, his hands swept over her shoulders, down her arms until his fingers clasped hers. He broke the kiss and smiled at her. He lifted her arms, placing one then the other above her head. He gazed into her eyes, at her lips, at her breasts. He shook his head slightly.

'So beautiful, Dani.' He shifted his hold on her, freeing one of his hands but keeping her wrists pinioned above her head by the other. He moved onto his side, one thigh still weighting hers but baring her body to his view.

He smiled as he gazed down her length again. And then his fingers followed his sightline. Coasting lightly down her body, caressing, teasing down her neck, her breasts, circling her belly button and then lower over her stomach, lower still…

Dani shifted restlessly, breathing faster.

'What?' he murmured in her ear. 'What do you want?'

She arched her spine in response, aching to feel all of him against her again. His fingers teased, twirling in her hot, wet space. She was so close to tipping over the edge—but it wasn't what she wanted. It wasn't all she wanted. She moaned, unable to stop the sound of pure frustration.

'Isn't this enough?' His words tickled her ear. 'Don't I just let my fingers do the walking, hmm? Isn't that what you do? Isn't this all you need? Better than a man, more reliable? Satisfying?'

She was so *unsatisfied*. 'Alex.' Even as she complained she tried to snuggle closer, wanting more of his body against her.

'So tell me, then, what you really want.' His fingers didn't stop teasing and she was beside herself. The ache widened inside; her body yearned to cushion his. To have him imprinted on her. *Inside* her.

But he didn't alter the slow, teasing touches—just kept them the same—keeping her right on the edge and not letting her go over.

She moved again, grinding into his hand, trying to force a

harder, faster stroke, but he just chuckled and kept it the same maddening torture.

The heat overwhelmed her. 'You want me to spell it out for you?'

'Yes.'

She whispered it in his ear—the same words she'd used this morning. The ones that had made him move so wickedly.

He rolled right on top of her, his knees pushing her legs further apart, and she nearly fainted with the blissful antici-pation of it. His thighs were heavy, strong. She hooked her feet back over his calves. Tangling with him was irresistible. And he was so close, she could feel the head of his erection pressing against her. She only had to lift her hips the slight-est and she'd have him. But he looked down at her, his eyes dark, and lifted his hips away—just enough.

His chest was squashing hers but she didn't mind. In fact, she loved the weight and the hardness of it—loved the feeling of being trapped beneath him. She arched, seeking. 'Alex.'

'What?' He pressed kisses to her neck, his body warming hers, his hand cupping, clasping.

'Don't tease me.'

'Who says I'm teasing?' His eyes glinted. 'Sex as good as this doesn't happen that often. You have to admit that.'

She looked up at him. Surprised into silence. So this was off the charts for him too? Her excitement ratcheted an im-possible degree higher.

His whole body flexed. He knew—he'd felt the tremor of response in her body. He lifted, repositioned, pressed even harder against her. 'You know how incredible this is, Dani.'

He thrust home and every last thought fled in the warmth of feeling that engulfed her.

'Tell me how it feels,' he asked, teeth gritted, body rigid.

She was so aware of his strength. The strength she now had inside her—barely leashed, about to burst through her. But it didn't frighten her. All the fear she'd had bottled inside for years had vanished in the instant he'd taken her, chased away by the absolute feeling of *rightness*.

'Good.' She managed to breathe—unable to be anything but honest. 'So good. So good.' So much better than good.

He released her wrists. She swept her hands over his back, tracing the muscles, and then stretched to clasp his shoulders, her fingers spread wide. She arched up to him—loving the heat and weight and power of him.

Staying slow wasn't something either of them could manage. The ability to form words faded, sighs sounded instead. Faster they moved. Pushing closer, rotating so the friction grew unbearable. And yet he had just enough discipline—changing the angle, watching her face, waiting those few minutes until she could no longer hold back. Her body went taut, every cell seizing, her breath caught for an endless moment. And then she convulsed— shuddering with the spasms of delight that ravaged through her.

His grip broke, his body freed to move as fast and hard as it craved to, his hands holding her so close and his groan gorgeously rough in her ears.

When she opened her eyes it was morning already and she was alone. Maybe she'd somehow staggered down to her own room during the night? How would she know? All she could remember was the way they'd moved together—how many times had it been? She blinked, shifting the all-too-delicious images from her head, and focused. No, this wasn't the spare room. This was his room. She slipped out of the bed gingerly, then made a dash for her bedroom. Saw it wasn't yet seven. Wow. He did rise early.

She showered, trying to soothe her still hypersensitive skin, and dressed. By the time she got to the kitchen he was in place—breakfast half eaten. He stood as soon as she appeared.

'I've got an omelette for you ready to go.'

'I can't eat a rich breakfast.'

'You need sustenance. You didn't get much sleep last night.'

Well, he'd had even less. 'What time did you get up?'

'I get up at five.'

'*Why?*' Madness. Especially on a Saturday.

His phone beeped and he flashed a grin. 'There are bankers awake in all twenty-four hours of the day. And people always want their questions answered *now*.'

Really? It was all work? She pointed at his phone. 'You just set this up to try to impress me. Make me think you're an amazingly committed worker.'

'You don't think I am?'

Of course she did. But she couldn't resist teasing him. 'First impressions, Alex. First time I saw you, you were wandering around the office like a butterfly—stopping to chat and smile and make the place pretty while the worker ants got it all done for you.'

He didn't seem remotely offended, just sent a lecherous look over her body. 'Want to know my first impression of you?'

'No.'

'Chicken.'

'I'm not biting.'

'No, that was my first impression of you. A little scaredy cat in the lift.'

She tilted her chin and called him on it. 'You'd been staring at me for days before the lift incident. That wasn't your first impression.'

His smile widened. 'My very first impression I can't say aloud. It wouldn't be gentlemanly.'

She flushed.

'And, no, that impression hasn't changed. In fact, it's been enhanced.' He gave her a playful pat on the rear. 'Now hurry up and eat—we've got to go help Lorenzo.'

Dani was sorely tempted to slap him back, but she suspected she'd end up beneath him if she did that and her body needed a couple of hours' recovery time first. 'Help him with what?'

'You'll see.'

Ten minutes later Dani watched out of the window as they drove out of the inner-city flash-apartment zone, through a commercial area and eventually into a much poorer residential area. 'How do you know each other?'

'Lorenzo?'

'Yeah.' They seemed an odd mix. Alex was so the outgoing charming kind whereas Lorenzo was definitely the silent brooder.

'We were at school together. Became friends there and have been ever since.'

So it was just the boys' network thing. 'And you set up the charity together?'

'Lorenzo had the idea but didn't want to be the public eye so much. He collared me for most of that. I wanted to support him.'

'Why did he want to do it?'

Alex sent her a quick glance. 'Lorenzo didn't have a great upbringing. He wants to help kids in a similar position.'

How not so great an upbringing? 'But you were at the same school?' Somehow she imagined Alex had gone to some exclusive number that cost lots of money and she suspected that when he said Lorenzo's upbringing hadn't been so great, he meant it had been lacking—in every way.

'Boarding school, yes. Lorenzo was a scholarship kid.'

'Boarding?' Dani lifted her brows. Alex was an only child

whose parents had lived in the biggest city in New Zealand—there were posh private schools practically on their doorstep.

'It was one of those boys' own schools out in the country—lots of physical endurance stuff to keep us out of trouble.'

'Don't tell me you got into trouble, Alex,' she teased.

His grin was twisted. 'Why do you think my mother sent me there?'

She didn't really believe him—this was Alex, the straight-up finance boss. But while he might be grinning, there was an edge of bitterness too—she wanted to ask more but he pulled the car to the kerb. 'Here we are.'

Dani took in the scene—the tools, the wood, the sign on the building. They were building a new fence for a playgroup?

'I'm happy to dig the last couple of holes for the side fence.' Alex slammed the door.

Lorenzo looked up from where he stood in the back of the truck, tossing out implements. 'You got energy to burn?'

'And then some.'

Dani stepped out of the car. OK, what was her role here?

'You mind raking the leaves, Dani?' Alex glanced over from where he was already picking up a spade.

'Sure.' She wasn't work-shy. Good thing too because it took her over an hour to rake up all the leaves from the paths and heap them into the green waste wheelie bins. Then she swept and pulled a few weeds. By then she was burning to make a cutting comment or two because this wasn't exactly her idea of Saturday-morning fun.

'Where are the cameras?' She stood alongside the fence line Alex was digging the post holes for. 'Don't you want your charity bit to be recorded for publicity?'

'This is just a little job we're doing on the quiet. We save the cameras for the big set pieces like the dinner the other night.' Alex leaned on the spade and drawled, 'When we're looking our handsomest.'

Dani could argue that one. Sure, he was to die for in a tux, but in faded old jeans and a tee shirt that was now clinging to his sweaty torso, well, hell. Officially it might be autumn, but as far as she was concerned it was hotter than Hades.

He was obviously used to a bit of physical work—could handle a spade and a wheelbarrow. But she couldn't sit here and watch him all day lugging wood and digging and looking way too manly. And it looked as if they were going to be doing this *all* day. Lorenzo had put up the horizontals on the front fence—where the posts had already been concreted in.

She picked up the bag of nails and interrupted Alex again. 'Give me a hammer.'

'Pardon?'

'A hammer.'

'I'm not sure that's such a good idea.' Alex stood back from his work. 'You've got such precious fingers, very little thumbs.'

'Lucky, aren't I? Means they're easy to miss,' she said smartly. 'What makes you think a girl can't hammer in a few nails?'

She'd done all the DIY in the little flat her mother and she had rented—well, as much of it as she could without doing worse damage. Plumbing was beyond her, but nailing up a few fence palings was a cinch. She went to the end of the fence and got started.

Alex had dug the last of the holes for the back fence and he and Lorenzo concreted the poles in. They'd obviously worked together a lot. And she wasn't noticing how good Alex looked grubby.

Finally they stopped for food. Alex magicked a hamper from in the boot of his car. Dani stared at the yummy pottles he was finding forks for.

He noticed her salivating, and his grin was too cocky. 'I know a great deli.'

'How come you two are so good at this?'

'Summers working on a farm. Fence post after fence post.' Alex handed her a pottle of pasta salad and a fork.

He'd spent his summers working? She was pleasantly surprised—would have thought a richer-than-rich playboy prince like him would have been off gallivanting round the globe every semester break. She looked at the perfectly straight fence posts. Nope, he was definitely experienced with this.

As soon as she filled the pit that was her stomach she turned her back and got on with her section. Banging in the nails was a rewarding way to burn off some of her energy. It was accruing again, in giant tubfuls—the desire to be with him.

'What makes *you* so good at this?'

She jumped. He was standing right beside her, tracing his finger along the palings where she'd hammered the nails in a neat row.

'Necessity.'

His brows lifted. 'Is there nothing you can't do all on your own, Dani?'

'Not a thing.' She slung the hammer back into the tool box, glanced up to see a frown on his face. 'What?'

He brushed the backs of his fingers along her jaw, slid them up to sweep that annoying bit of fringe back. 'Are you sure about that?'

His tone was different—loaded with meaning. He wasn't teasing her. It wasn't a reference to the way he'd played with her in bed last night. His eyes held none of that heat; instead it was all seriousness, all concern.

Eli.

Her heart started thundering. If she asked Alex to help, it would happen. He would find him. And wasn't that what she wanted more than anything in the world? Suddenly she was scared. Really, really scared of what she might find. And too scared not to search. She watched, distracted, as Alex and Lorenzo loaded the rest of the gear on the truck, then all three stood for a moment and admired the pristine fence.

Alex shot Lorenzo a look. 'Tempted?'

'Like you wouldn't believe.'

Alex laughed. 'Bad boy. Come back for a drink instead.'

Dani saw Lorenzo glance from Alex to her and then back to Alex. 'Not today, thanks.'

Once they were in the car she just had to ask. 'What was he tempted to do?'

Alex grinned. 'Renz liked to tag as a teen.'

'Graffiti?' Dani's brows lifted. 'Did you help him get on the straight and narrow?'

'Are you kidding?' Alex laughed. 'I got him the paint.'

He disappeared upstairs when they got home. Dani's body had seized up in the car; it was all she could do to hobble to the kitchen. She got ice-cold water from the fridge and carefully sat on a stool.

'Tired?'

Warm fingers slid beneath her tee shirt and walked up her spine.

'Yes.'

'Come on.' He sounded husky.

Heaven help her, she thought she might be too tired even to manage that. He chuckled and picked her up, easily loping up the stairs with her. He went straight through his bedroom to the en-suite bathroom adjacent to it.

'Oh.' She blinked.

There were candles lit everywhere—tons of them, all different sizes, but all that gorgeous deep red, and her favourite berrylicious scent. Out of the window the autumnal sky was closing in, a blue-grey that darkened with every beat of her heart.

'Alex…' She looked up at him, registered his slightly smug smile, and his arms tightened. She put on a pout and shook her head. 'Don't think this is going to get you any extra points.'

'I don't need any more points.' He grinned and then tipped her into the bath, clothes and all. She went right under and emerged with a splutter, sending fluffy white bubbles everywhere. She knelt up and looked at him, watched as he yanked his shirt off his head. Sinking back into the delicious, almost-too-hot water, she melted as he scuffed off his jeans. Heaven.

He laughed as she sighed, stepped into the bath behind her. Oh, yes. He didn't need any more points. She turned to face him and he pulled her close, the tips of his fingers making patterns with the bubbles on her skin. 'Wet tee shirt.' His eyes gleamed. 'Nice.'

'You're a gentleman and a rogue, Alex Carlisle.'

He blew some of the bubbles from her arm. 'What makes you say that?'

'You do this—' she waved a froth-covered hand at the flickering candles that cast a warm glow in the room '—set it up so beautifully and then you dunk me in fully clothed.'

He leaned back, water streaming over his bronzed body emphasising the lean, hard muscles, and his brows flicked up and down. 'Irresistible impulse.'

'Succumb to them often, do you?'

'Around you. Yes.'

She gazed at him, experiencing a rather irresistible impulse of her own as his silky-smooth words washed over her with that undertone of laughter as the chaser.

Utterly irresistible.

She rose to her knees, leant forward and gave him a gentle kiss on the cheek. 'Thank you.'

Lifting far enough away to focus, she saw a curious expression in his eyes.

'I'm glad you like it,' he murmured.

'You remembered the candle from the hostel.'

He nodded.

'You're very good with details.'

The curve of his mouth deepened.

She leant closer to him again, her voice merely a hot breath by his ear. 'What else are you good at?'

He inclined his head just that touch so his faintly stubbled jaw brushed her cheek. 'You sure you want to find out?'

'Absolutely.'

What felt like hours later she was finally naked and her muscles utterly slack, her legs floating in front of her as she used Alex like a lilo. She didn't think she'd ever felt so relaxed. The tiredness swamped her—the long months of hard work and heartbreak as she'd cared for her slowly dying mother were finally taking their toll. The devastation at her father's callous abuse of them. What kind of person stole at a time like that?

Dani would give anything to have her back. Just anything. But there was nothing she could do. Except the one last thing she'd asked. Maybe she could bring peace to her mother's final rest—and peace for herself.

She was too tired, too desperate, not to take the help Alex had offered. Her pride in her independence had to be shelved. 'What you said yesterday…'

'About the investigator?'

She felt the reverberations in his chest as he spoke—even as softly as he had—and felt reassured by the solid strength of him.

'Yes.'

His wide palms stroked down her upper arms. 'You don't have to tell me about it. I can just make the appointment for you.'

She smiled sadly. He was offering her privacy, offering her help, but she wanted to share it now—it was a burden that had got too heavy for her, but that would be nothing to him. 'My mother had a son eight years before she had me. Here in New Zealand. She named him Eli. She adopted him out.'

'And you want to find him.'

She nodded. 'We've never met. He doesn't know I exist. I only found out about him just before she died. I only have the vaguest details and I've tried, but I can't get anywhere.'

'You don't have any other family, do you?'

She shook her head—none that she recognised.

'The PI will help.' Alex sounded all CEO certain. 'We'll call him tonight.'

'It's Saturday.'

'They work all hours.'

Like him. Unless he was in party mode. 'Shouldn't you be going out somewhere?'

'Nowhere else I'd rather be than here.'

Dani rested her head back on his chest and smiled at his hot-chocolate-smooth words—he always had the right answers, didn't he? But now, having told him about her search, she felt her exhaustion quadruple. She closed her eyes.

'Don't worry, Dani.' She heard him from a distance. 'We'll find him for you.'

CHAPTER NINE

DANI looked up at Alex's deep sigh.

He'd laid his cutlery down and his smile curved lopsidedly. 'We have to go out tonight.'

'We do?' She nearly choked on her last mouthful. He'd picked her up from work bang on time, spun her in his arms the minute they got to the top of the stairs of his house, kissed her while walking them through to the kitchen and made the most of the big bench. When they'd finally come up for air and done their clothes back up, they'd sat down to dinner. All she wanted to do now was fall into bed—and play some more.

Yesterday had been divine—according to Alex the 'day of rest' meant no getting out of bed all day. In between the ferocious sex they'd dozed, she'd read the newspapers, he tapped on his laptop and they'd snacked on whatever they could find in the fridge. She was still hot from it—and exhausted in equal measure.

'Drinks with the charity divas. It won't take long but I need to put in an appearance.'

'I don't, though.'

'Yes, you do, you're the newest employee and they're all

very keen to meet you. Besides, you're my excuse to leave early. You'll have a headache.'

'What? No way. You can have your own headache.' She watched him clear the plates. 'Do we have to dress up?' She didn't want to take up his offer to buy her some clothes—an offer he'd repeated in the guise of a loan—but the fact was, apart from a few work skirts and shirts and her one little black dress, it was jeans and tee and that was it.

'Casual is fine.'

But after a quick shower she put on one of her quality cotton work shirts, tucking it into her jeans and securing them with a belt. She pulled on her boots instead of the trainers she preferred to jog round in when she was doing 'casual'. Her casual and his casual were two quite different things. As a last touch she slid in the clip he'd given her the night of the dance. There were a couple of other women in jeans, Dani noted when they got there, but their jeans were designer.

It was a much smaller gathering than the dinner had been, much more informal and much more intimidating. The dinner had been too busy and too loud for any real in-depth conversation with anyone. This was more like appearing in front of a selection panel for an elite club. She was sure she was being judged—and that she was failing.

Alex held her hand and she was grateful for that because, beneath the tastefully mascaraed lashes, she was getting a few scarily close looks. The princesses of society all seemed to have gathered together and now they inspected her with barely veiled curiosity. She made her head stay up high; she would not drop it and stare at the floor. But she was nothing like them—she didn't have the breeding, the elite education, the looks, definitely not the wardrobe. His fingers gripped hers tighter and she sensed him looking at her.

She met the look and murmured softly in his ear, 'How many of the women in this room have you slept with?'

'Not even a tenth of how many you're thinking.' He lifted her hand to his chest, pressing it against the fine merino sweater so she could feel the steady beat of his heart, and grinned broadly at her. 'Not feeling insecure, are you?'

'Oh, no.' Hers was going machine-gun–style.

He grinned. 'They just want to get to know you.'

More like they just wanted her out of the way so they could get to him. Now she understood why his arrogance was so innate. People thought he was wonderful—they just about bowed and scraped as he made his way across the room. And now they were doing the same for her—granting her a kind of power just because of her perceived association with him. Except for her they had sharp eyes, even sharper smiles. She didn't fit in and they knew it.

She looked around desperately as Alex chatted to an older couple. Another jeans-clad woman stood across the room, alone and on the outer. The thoughts so readable on her face mirrored the ones inside Dani—she wanted to get the hell out of there.

Dani murmured an 'excuse me' and walked towards her, ignoring Alex's movement to keep her close.

'Hello,' Dani introduced herself to the woman. 'I'm Dani.'

'Sara.' The woman smiled shyly. 'It's my first time.'

'Me too.' Dani gave her a look and both their smiles went wider. 'What brings you here?'

'I'm representing one of the charities the fund is considering supporting. I'm doing a presentation at next week's board meeting and they invited me along tonight so I could meet some of the board members. To break the ice.'

Well, the ice was shatterproof in some corners of the room.

'Tell me about your charity.' Dani grinned. 'You can practise on me.'

It was so nice to talk about someone and something else for five minutes. Dani was tired of smiling and 'mmming' and 'ahhing' and trying not to give her secrets away. They took a drink from a passing waiter and bonded.

Every so often Alex would glance across to her and she saw the keen question in his eye—not so much an 'are you OK?' kind of caring question, but a 'what are you up to?' keen observance. She turned her back on him and made herself relax. Another charity worker joined them, then another, and they found chairs and talked about their projects.

'How's your head, Dani?' Alex bobbed down behind her seat and enquired—all seeming solicitude.

'It's fine.' She smiled brightly, deliberately missing the message in his eyes. 'Honestly, that delicious dinner really seemed to do the trick. I feel so much better than I did an hour or so ago.'

She turned back to Sara and the other women sitting beside her and smiled. 'So tell me more.'

Sara's cheeks were deep pink as she looked from Dani to Alex and back again. 'Are you sure you have time?'

'I have all the time in the world.' Dani looked up and smiled sweetly at the tall man towering beside her. 'Don't I?'

'Of course.' His smile was set charm, then he walked off.

Dani beamed at Sara, savouring the moment—she did like to tease him.

Another half-hour passed and she was engrossed in conversation. Well, almost engrossed—her Alex-radar was as on as ever. She was aware of him watching her almost stalker-like. And she lifted her head when he approached again—with unmistakable purpose.

'I'm very sorry to interrupt, Dani—' Alex broke through the circle of chairs and held his hand out to her '—but it really is time for us to go.'

'You haven't met Sara—'

'Alex Carlisle.' Alex immediately turned and took Sara's hand instead. Shaking it briefly. Then he wrapped his arm around Dani's shoulders and literally hauled her to her feet.

'I'm sorry I've talked at you all evening.' Sara stood too.

'Not at all,' Dani reassured her with a genuine grin. 'I really enjoyed hearing about it.'

He didn't drag the goodbyes to the hostess and Dani was so amused by his impatience she was able to rise above the cool nods she got from some of the queens.

Outside they walked to where he'd parked.

'You meant it, didn't you?' Alex unlocked the car.

'Meant what?'

'That you enjoyed hearing about Sara's work.'

Dani slid into the seat. 'So what if I did?'

His smile broadened. 'And you can be so nice to people. So social.'

'I'm house-trained too,' she said witheringly. 'Isn't that an advantage?'

His smile gave way to laughter then.

'Well, really, Alex, what did you think—that I'd sit there sullen and stupid all night?'

'No, but nor did I expect you to have half the room hanging on your every word and have them falling over each other to talk to you.'

'That wasn't me,' she said acidly. 'That was my status. Walking in with Alex Carlisle, I couldn't be anything but a success.'

'Why do you insist on hiding behind a wall of sarcasm

from even the vaguest compliment?' He accelerated. 'Dani, it was you. I've seen far more famous women, far more supposedly *important* women, fail to have anything like that effect on a group like that. You charmed them.'

'I didn't. I just talked to them.' Dani fidgeted with the side seam of her jeans. 'Why were you in such a rush to leave, anyway?'

'I want you.'

OK, that was to the point and something of a relief given the lust she was grappling with. Even so, she couldn't resist a tease. 'But I have a headache, *remember*?'

Alex dragged himself away from her warm, sleepy body, showered and dressed. Made himself a nuclear-strength coffee and forced the bitterness down his throat. He needed the caffeine hit. He powered up the computer on the desk overlooking the garden, then checked his phone. There were five messages waiting. He scrolled and then stilled. One was from Patrick, which he ignored. One was from the investigator.

Alex didn't care how early it was, he was paying the man enough to be able to call him any time—even two hours before dawn. The guy was impressively lucid considering he'd just been woken—but there wasn't much to report. Nothing on Dani's brother. Not good enough.

'Where else can you look? There must be something, right?'

He was increasingly determined to find him for her. The investigator explained the problem—when searching the birth records, Dani's mother's name wasn't coming up anywhere, which meant that at the time of her son's adoption the original birth certificate was sealed. So, without a court order, the only person who can access the full details on the certificate is that child himself—no one else, not even his sister. The investigator needed to find him through other means. He asked if Alex knew any more details.

'No. I don't have more details—no date, no photo, no nothing. There can't have been that many babies adopted out that year. Check the ones before and after. Just find him.' He jabbed the end button and tossed it in the bench. Damn.

A faint sound alerted him. Whirling round, he saw her—in the doorway, her wide eyes searching his, so full of fearful hope. Alex winced. He wasn't big on bursting bubbles for people. And so he did it quick—less painful that way, right?

'There's nothing yet, sorry, Dani. It's not looking good.'

For a moment she did nothing, the shock etched on her face. She believed he could help, didn't she? Frustration burned hotter inside him. He wanted to be able to. He wanted to smooth away that pinched look—to sweep the pain from her eyes. He moved. But she did too—turning her back to him.

'I'm going to make breakfast.' She opened the fridge. 'Pizza. Sounds weird, I know, but it's the only thing I can cook. You've got ready-made bases in here. I saw them the other day. Spinach and egg. Some people think it's gross but I love it.'

Alex said nothing, just stood on the other side of the bench and watched her sudden burst of busyness. She put the bases, spinach, eggs and cheese down. Found his biggest knife.

'Do you have pasta sauce? I need some pasta sauce.'

Hell, she looked tired. And suddenly he too felt exhausted. Maybe they should both just go back to bed—to sleep.

By now she had the board. The green leaves were under the guillotine.

'Dani.' He risked life and limb and put his hand on hers. 'We'll do everything to find him for you, I promise. Everything.' He applied more pressure to his grip. 'You can trust me, OK?'

'Sure.' The knife hit the board.

Bang, bang, bang.

No more talking. She wouldn't look at him. She wasn't going to let him in on it—her disappointment, her fear, her hurt. And that made him almost as disappointed himself.

His phone beeped again and he wanted to chuck it in the waste-disposal unit. He wanted to help her. Wanted her to have the success that he hadn't—to find the happiness she wanted. Instead he was rendered useless.

When he looked up from tapping out a message she'd abandoned the spinach. 'I don't feel like pizza anymore.' She put the knife down. 'What a mess.'

'The housekeeper will take care of it.'

But she wasn't talking about that mess and he knew it.

Her shoulders slumped. 'I'm sorry the search is taking up your time, Alex. I know you have more important things to be doing.'

Was that defeat he'd just heard from her? He saw the way her fingers trembled as she tucked her hair behind her ear. Well, that wasn't right. He wanted the strong, sassy Dani back.

'You mean, you think I actually do important things?' He tried to tease her out. 'I thought I was only about swanning around and seducing the nearest available woman.'

'OK, I admit that when you've done your seducing for the day you might put some effort into your work, as well.'

Clearly she was not herself.

'Why, thank you.' He walked to her side of the bench, determined to bring the sparkle back to her eyes. 'But you're mistaken about something.'

'I am?' She finally looked at him. 'What?'

'I'm never done with seducing for the day.' He smiled down at her. Then his smile stuttered as he saw how the pain came from right inside her, her big brown eyes dulled with sorrow and uncertainty.

He wound his arms around her and pulled her close for a plain old-fashioned hug, tempering the desire that surged every time he got within three feet of her, pressing her head into his shoulder so he didn't have to see that hurt anymore, because somehow it hurt him. And he wanted to pretend he really was helping somehow.

'It's going to be OK, Dani.' It was all he could think of to say. And it wasn't enough. He couldn't guarantee her anything, but in this moment it didn't stop him trying.

Dani figured she must be the worst temp ever. She hadn't been paying any attention to what Cara had been saying. All she could think about was the news Alex had relayed. The disappointment was overwhelming. *Nothing.* No leads—no possibilities. She might never find Eli. She might never get to tell him how sorry their mother was—how she'd thought of him every day—how she'd wanted to love him. Dani might never find her family. The thoughts cut her heart. She had to focus on something else—like answering letters or inputting numbers. But futility drummed a relentless beat—she wasn't going to do it; she wasn't going to be able to do it for her mother.

And the follow-on questions grew louder and louder in her head—if she wasn't going to find her brother, why was she still here? How much longer did she give Alex's PI to find him? How much longer would she let herself be with Alex?

For the first question the answer was easy—they had to have more time. She hadn't packed up and moved countries to give up after only a few weeks. She wouldn't let them stop. Somewhere someone must be able to help—surely they'd find him eventually.

As for Alex, he was just part of the deal, wasn't he? The physical favour. Hardly—she mocked herself. No way was it 'just sex' and uncomplicated—it already was complicated for her. Half her heart was his. And he hadn't asked for it. How she wished he would.

'Did the meeting run late last night?'

She finally heard Cara. 'Oh. Not too bad, no.'

'Oh.' Cara smiled. 'You seem a little tired today. Distracted.'

Dani felt her cheeks warm. 'I'm sorry.'

'It's OK,' Cara said. 'There's not much to do today anyway.'

Dani's mobile rang.

'I'll send a taxi to pick you up this afternoon.' Alex got straight to the point. 'I have a thing I have to go to. I forgot to mention it this morning.'

'Sure. No problem.' So he didn't need his 'date' for this one. Dani battled against feeling disappointed but lost. Nor could she control the feeling of concern from rising—he'd sounded tired, which was unusual. She wished she could see him—to read his expression—because something had definitely been off.

Silly. She reminded herself with hard words—she wasn't his mother, or his girl, not even a friend. She was his flatmate with fringe benefits. That was all.

'That was Alex?' Cara asked.

Dani nodded, knew her colour was rising.

'Gorgeous, isn't he?' Cara sparkled. 'He and Lorenzo are the most eligible bachelors in town—and not because of their bank balances or bodies. Although—' she looked coy '—I don't know that Alex is going to be a bachelor for much longer.'

Dani looked at Cara with great concern. 'Can I get you a cup of tea or some cold water?' Pregnancy was making the poor woman delusional.

Alone in his house, she found some ready-made soup in the fridge, ate it while standing. She sloped up to bed early. But despite feeling exhausted she couldn't sleep. She went back downstairs and curled up on the sofa—but she couldn't settle into a book, decide on a telly channel, or choose a movie. It was the tone she kept hearing—that discordant note in his voice when he'd rung. She couldn't sleep until she'd seen him.

She heard the gates and the garage door. He wasn't nearly as late as she'd thought he'd be. She listened to his slow, heavy tread on the stairs and waited. He appeared in the doorway and shock rippled through her. She sat up. 'What's wrong?'

He looked awful—his face all shadows and angles. And as he stepped further into the room she saw the shadows were darkened by something else—pain. He looked at her, his expression so tortured that the vulnerability struck a knife in her heart. She couldn't believe this wreck of a man was Alex. Usually full of such vitality. She'd never thought he could look so destroyed.

'Tell me.' She needed to know. She needed to help.

But he was silent.

Her cheeks heated. He didn't want to tell her. Was she overstepping the mark? Too bad. She reverted to blunt speak. 'You look awful.'

A little puff of air escaped him and he flopped onto the sofa beside her. He closed his eyes, his brows knitting. Then suddenly he spoke. 'I had a meeting with my father.'

Dani blinked. That she hadn't expected. 'But—'

'Samuel Carlisle wasn't my father.'

Oh—Dani thought it but no sound came out of her mouth. Instead she sat utterly still. And waited.

'I always knew my parents weren't that happy. It wasn't fights all the time or anything. It was just…chilly. Then I heard my mother one day on the phone. I was only twelve but I wasn't naive. It was an argument with her lover. I walked in to where she was and she hung up straight away. I asked her and she denied it, tried to laugh it off. But I knew. And I never told Samuel because I knew it would freak him.'

He went silent. 'After that I went to boarding school. I was still close to Samuel, but not her. I went to university, went into the business. Then Da…' he paused '…*Samuel* got sick. He needed a donor. She didn't want me to be tested—said I was too young. But I did it anyway. The blood work came through. I'm a really rare type. I looked it up, and Samuel's— had them checked. There was no way he could be my father.'

Dani bit down on her lips as she watched his pallor increase.

'I confronted her—she admitted it but begged me not to tell him. To him I was his only child. It would kill him.' He sighed. 'So I didn't, of course. But I wanted to know the truth. She wouldn't say—said his name was irrelevant. Nothing more than a sperm donation. Insisted Samuel was my real father.'

'And wasn't he?' Dani asked softly. 'In every way that counted?'

He turned his head and looked at her. 'I had the right to know. Samuel had the right to know.'

That was true. She nodded—she understood the need to know.

'She died before she ever told me who my father really was. I could never ask Samuel. So I thought I'd never find out. Samuel lived for a few more years—desperately sick, desperate to see the bank succeed. So I made it succeed.'

The silence was long. And eventually Dani prompted him. 'And then he died.

'And almost a year to the day I got the call.'

Dani's mind searched for the answer and then made the stabbing guess. 'Patrick.'

'So obvious now, isn't it?' His smile was faint and bitter. 'He was their best man, can you believe that? He used to be like an uncle—always around when I was a kid. Now I know why. After she died he moved to Singapore—for business, apparently. He's been there since. Never married. He insists the affair ended years before, but how can I believe a word he says? And now he wants a *relationship*.' He turned and stared at Dani. 'How can you have a relationship with someone when they've done nothing but lie to you all your life?'

He screwed his face up. 'How could they? It could have been found out so much sooner if I'd ever been seriously sick. She ran the risk of it for years. But she never said anything. All my life I had the Carlisle duty drummed into me.' His anger mounted. 'The bank. The business. It was my destiny—rammed into me.'

'What else would you have done?'

'I've no idea. I never seriously thought about it. It just was. Even Patrick advised me to go into it—when he was doing his honorary uncle bit.'

'But you're good at your job, Alex. You enjoy it. No one could work the kind of hours you do if they didn't enjoy it.'

'You think? What about all those people who work two, three, four jobs just to get food on the table? It's about necessity, Dani. And it was necessary for me. Samuel was sick—he was dying and the company hit the skids. I had to turn it round—rescue it while he was alive to see it saved. I had to prove to everyone that I was good enough to do it—that I deserved to be the boss, not just because I was his heir. I did it all for him. For her. And she'd lied to me. For years and years she lied.'

Betrayal. It hurt so much when a parent let you down. Dani understood that too.

He shook his head. 'My whole life has been a lie, Dani.'

She looked at the tension etched into his face and took his hand in hers. 'When did he call?'

'Thursday, almost two weeks ago.'

The day before he'd kissed her. Now she understood why he had. He'd been having a rough time and gone for a moment of fun. And, boy, had he got a whole lot more than he'd bargained for. Poor Alex.

His anger rippled out again. 'I insisted on tests. But it's true.' His fingers tightened unbearably on hers but she held in the wince, knowing he wasn't aware of his strength. 'Why should I have anything to do with him?'

'People lie for all sorts of reasons, Alex. I'm not saying it's right, but maybe you need to ask what those reasons might be.'

'There's no excuse.'

'People lie to protect—sometimes themselves, sure, but sometimes to protect others too. Maybe they lied to protect you. They didn't want to hurt you.'

'Protect me from what? Not knowing hurt more, Dani.' He lifted his hands from her and looked at them. 'I used to wonder if she'd been raped.'

'Alex.' Her heart wrenched and she grabbed his hands again with both of hers and pulled them to her chest. Of course he'd have worried about the worst. Afraid of what his mother's secrecy might have meant.

He looked at her, tormented. 'And they let me wonder. Worry. For nothing. I can't forgive them for that.' The deepest hurt poured out. 'He's despicable, Dani. I don't want anything to do with him. I can't believe he's my father. I don't want to be related to him.'

She had to reach out to him. She had to help somehow, because she understood that hatred—and the underlying fear that the badness might come through his blood.

'I've lied to you too, Alex,' she said quietly. It wasn't even a lie that would affect him, yet she felt terrible for it. Even more so as she felt him freeze. 'I told you my parents were dead,' she said quickly. 'And my mum is but my father isn't.'

Silent, he stared at her.

She breathed in and then said it. The one thing she tried never to think about. 'He's in jail.'

'Oh—'

'As far as I'm concerned he died the day he came to see Mum when she was dying of cancer and conned the last of her life savings from her.' Dani spoke fast, stopping his interruption. She wasn't telling him this to get his sympathy, but so he'd grasp what she wanted him to learn. 'He's a crook, Alex. A conman—theft, fraud, you name it, he's done it. The kind of lowlife who preys on the sick and dying.' She hated him, hated the way her heart raced and her skin went cold when she thought of him. 'He wandered in and out of our lives—between sentences, between better options. He'd come and sweet talk his way back to Mum, saying he was changed. Always lies. Right up to the end, he stole from her. He has no conscience, no empathy, nothing.' And she'd wanted to believe him too, hadn't she? Every time. So not only had he stolen from her mother, he'd stolen from her too—taken her credit card and maxed it out. She let go of Alex's hand to push back the sweep of her fringe. 'His blood runs through my veins, Alex, but I'm not like him,' she said fiercely. 'I'm not anything like him.' She spoke faster, insistent. 'It doesn't matter who your biological parents are. You're still you. You're not him. You'll never be him.'

Alex just kept staring at her. 'Is it that easy to accept, Dani?'

'No,' she said honestly. 'But you have to. We're unique, right? It's our experiences that shape us, not just our DNA.'

'Yeah.' His smile was a shadow of its usual self, but at least it appeared. For all of a second. Then he went serious again. 'Wow.' He paused. 'Thanks for telling me.'

She scrunched deeper into the sofa. 'I don't like to think about him.'

'No.' He'd gone pale again, staring at the low coffee table in front of them, looking too tired to move.

'I guess you have to decide whether you want anything to do with Patrick,' she said softly.

Alex shook his head slowly. 'I don't want to know him.'

'That's OK, Alex.' She smiled at him a little sadly. 'You don't have to.' She held his hand, her heart aching for the hurt in his. 'Your phone hasn't beeped.' It must be a record.

He jerked. 'Oh, I turned it off. I'd better check it.'

'Give it to me.'

Their eyes met. Silently he handed it to her. She didn't look at it, most certainly didn't switch it on. She put it on the arm of the sofa.

Two disappointed people. Couldn't they forget the past for a few hours? Abandon the search for answers? Just breathe and let rest soothe the aches they both had. She reached forward and unlaced his shoes. 'You're tired. You need to get some sleep.'

Neither of them had had a decent night's sleep all week. She took his hand and stood, tugged until he drew his feet in and stood too. She let him up the stairs—past her landing and on up to his bedroom. She undid his tie, his buttons on his shirt, his trousers, slid them from his body. 'Lie down.'

He got into the bed. 'I want you to stay.'

'I am.' In her pink-pig pjs she joined him.

'I—'

'Just go to sleep, Alex.' She put her arms around him. Hugged him close. Cared for him.

CHAPTER TEN

Alex didn't want to move—couldn't. Way too content. Dani lay beside him, curling into him, warming him more comfortably than the softest wool blanket. And now nothing else did matter. Because just resting together like this was so complete. The questions faded, the need for answers, and the bitterness disappeared the way wisps of clouds did beneath the heat of the sun—just, like, that.

All that he needed right now was right here.

In the early morning he looked across at her. Still asleep, she looked so beautiful. He'd never seen anyone so beautiful. And he wanted to see her happy. He wanted to see her have some fun—and not just *that* kind of fun. His heart leapt up, somersaulted, and bellyflopped back into his chest. He was *interested*—in her and everything about her. The caring she'd shown last night had melted something inside him. Her telling him that about her father…he knew that had been hard. He knew how private she was, how protective. But she'd done it because she'd thought it might help him. And it had in more ways than she'd expect. It had made him see clearer—see *her* clearer. Now he needed to know even more. He needed to know everything—why she was so alone and what she hoped would happen when she found her brother.

He slipped out of bed. First he had to shower and get down to the office so he could make plans. But some of the peace from last night remained in his system. He felt freer somehow—less angsty about Patrick. He couldn't even think his relaxed state was from fantastic sex—they hadn't even had sex last night. Sharing a trouble—was it as simple as that? He glanced back to the sweet dreamer in his bed. No. It wasn't that simple. Not at all.

Alex appeared just before lunchtime, wearing jeans and tee. Dani stared—shouldn't he be at work?

'Come on.' He grinned. 'We're bunking.'

She gestured to the pile of letters in the tray on her desk. 'I can't.'

'Cara won't mind, will you, Cara?' He magnified the impact of his smile with a wink.

'Course not. Go on, Dani.'

'Where are we going?' she asked as soon as they were out of earshot.

He led her to his car. 'I realised that you've only been in New Zealand a couple of weeks and all you've done is work. You haven't had much fun.'

He was certainly in a play mood. She looked sideways at him—he was a different person from the tired, hurt man she'd seen last night. Now he was all colour and charm again. Her heart lifted and the smile bubbled out of her. 'So what we are doing?'

'It's a surprise.'

Dani felt excitement tingle in her tummy. So much for keeping her life free from getting more complicated. Complicated wasn't anywhere near enough of a description of her life—especially her *feelings* now.

'I brought your jeans and trainers. You might want to get changed.'

She wriggled in the passenger seat of his car, slipping off her skirt, laughing at his all too frequent glances towards her. 'Concentrate on the road!'

He pulled up near a big sports field. There were a couple of buses already stopped on the side of the road; the sound of people chattering carried through the trees.

'It's a rec afternoon for one of the Whistle Fund's beneficiary schools. They need some help with the kids.' He sent her an embarrassed kind of glance. 'Not that great a surprise, I guess. You up for it?'

She looked ahead through the trees to the football fields where orange cones were being set up and kids in trackies and trainers milled in a kind of amorphous mass. 'Sure, I like exercise.'

'I know.' His grin was pure shark.

She turned and went faux school marm on him in retaliation. 'But aren't you going to get behind with your work?'

'I can catch up tonight.'

And he would—the man worked round the clock. 'Admit it.' She poked him in the ribs with her finger.

'What?'

'You love it. There's nothing else you enjoy more than your wheeling and dealing. You're a banking and business geek. And you'd be lost without it.'

His eyes slid sideways. 'OK, I like it.'

'No.' She maintained her authoritarian tone. 'You *love* it.' He did—she'd *seen* him at work. He was happy there.

'OK, I love it.' He sighed and smiled at the same time. 'But I also like bunking now and then too.'

Yeah, but being the head of the family bank was his natural home—whether he was bloodstock or not. He was good at it too.

They walked over to where the few adults were being

sorted by the whistle-wearing coach. 'Skills and drills first, then games later.'

The kids were broken up into groups of eight and they worked them out—practising passes, forward and back, running games, short drills, team building.

Dani laughed—working her group while surreptitiously watching Alex work his crew just alongside her. His time at his 'boys' own outdoors' school was evident and it was equally clear he must work out a lot still—but then she knew that already.

She wasn't totally useless herself—she'd enjoyed her self-defence classes and working out at the gym. She might be on the curvy side, but that didn't mean she wasn't fit. She jumped up and caught a ball someone accidentally lobbed into the middle of her kids.

'Good catch,' Alex murmured. 'Nice to see a woman who isn't afraid of balls.'

'I *like* playing with them,' she answered, all soft sass and an oh-so-innocent smile.

He chuckled, shaking his head at their lame innuendo. She giggled too and got on with exercising her group for the best part of an hour—catching his eye too often and sharing that smile.

But the best bit was when the games of touch rugby began. A lightweight version of the thump-you-to-the-ground national sport—only in this you disarmed your opponent with a touch, not a tackle. Dani shouted encouragement to the kids whom she'd helped drill. Another hour slipped by until there was a grand winning team. Alex strolled over to where she was standing, applauding them with her gang.

'The winners want to play the leaders,' he said. 'You keen?'

'Absolutely.'

Some of the kids weren't that little and Dani felt her competitive spirit kick in. She looked along the field at Alex. They were on the same team. It was a nice feeling.

The game was fast, fun. Early on she got the ball, passed it straight to him and watched him run—all sleek speed and power. The try was easily scored.

The kids stood no chance against him.

At the end of it Dani asked him, 'You wouldn't let them win?'

Alex laughed and shook his head. 'It's good to learn how to lose. Besides, they wouldn't respect us if we didn't play an honest, hard-out game.'

He was right, of course. Except Dani wasn't sure he'd ever had to learn how to lose. She walked with him to where the coach was looking harassed. Now it was all over, some of the kids were tired and heading towards cranky.

'We'll load the shed,' Alex said. 'You guys head back. It'll be easier if Dani and I do it when you're all gone.'

The coach hesitated for all of half a second. 'Thanks.' He immediately started rounding everyone up—ordering them back to the buses.

'Bye, Alex.' One of the young players from his group hovered near.

'See ya.' Alex grinned and waved before turning to gather more of the gear and head towards the shed.

Dani looked at the young teen, saw how her round eyes swallowed Alex whole, how the colour swept into her cheeks before she turned and ran away. Dani smiled; she knew just how overwhelmed the poor girl felt.

'I'll repack the shed, you hand the stuff through to me.' Alex was already in there.

'Thanks.' She didn't fancy the job of being inside that windowless shack.

They worked quickly—Dani stacking the cones and

tossing the balls through to him. It took no time in the space and silence the rowdy kids had left. She waited outside the door while he put the remaining items away.

'Why do you feel trapped in enclosed spaces?' he asked from inside the shed. 'What happened?'

She spun the last ball between her hands. It wasn't a small space putting her on edge now.

'Tell me.' He stuck his head out of the door. 'Something happened, right? You got a fright some time.'

It was a long time ago and she tried never to think about it. 'It was nothing. I was an idiot.'

'What was nothing?'

No one but her mother knew what had happened that day. No one but him, of course. 'I'm not telling.'

He took the ball from her. 'Why not?'

'Because it was nothing.'

'It obviously was *not*,' he said with feeling, tossing the ball home. He shut the door and fixed the padlock, then moved to tower over her. 'Look, if you don't tell me, I'll hold you on the brink of orgasm for so long you won't be able to walk for three weeks because your body will be so sore from the strain of wanting it, but not getting it.'

She couldn't help but giggle at that. 'Sounds great—when do we start?'

'Tell me.'

Dani sighed. So he wasn't going to give up. Well, she'd give him the abridged version. 'I locked myself in a cupboard when I was fourteen. Was stuck in there for ages.' She forced another laugh—but it was too high-pitched.

'Why on earth did you do that?'

OK, so here was the not-so-fun part. She hesitated and felt him lean closer to her.

'Dani…' A very gentle warning.

'My mother's boyfriend came round. She was at work. She used to give her boyfriends a key,' Dani blurted—sooner said, sooner forgotten. 'I didn't like the way he looked at me.'

'So you hid from him?'

'He came into the house and called my name—he must have known Mum was at work so I went into my wardrobe. I heard him come into my room. He poked around everything. I was too scared to move. He stayed for ages. Until I couldn't tell if he was still there or not.'

All she'd been able to hear was the pounding of her heart. And her ears had hurt with the effort she'd had them under—waiting for the tiniest sound, terrified he was lurking just on the other side of the door and was going to smash it open at any moment.

And she'd been right.

'What happened?'

'He tried to break down the door.' Dani flinched, lost back in the memory of it. Barely aware she'd answered.

'*What?*'

Heart galloping, she turned to stare at Alex. Her body trembling with remembered shock. 'He knew I was there. He knew. And he waited and waited and waited until he got sick of waiting. And then he smashed the door.'

Alex swore. 'What did you do?'

'At first I couldn't do anything. I just couldn't move and I thought he was going to, to…but then the scream came out. I screamed and screamed.' But that moment—that infinite moment when she'd been unable to make a noise—had been the root of nightmares for years after.

'Did he get you? Did he hurt you?'

She shook her head. A couple of bruises from a couple of punches was nothing on what she could have suffered. 'The neighbour came over, she banged on the door and threatened to call the cops. He shoved her out of the way and ran off.'

'Did you go to the police?'

'No.' They'd been too scared for that. 'We changed the locks. Then we moved. But it wasn't that long before she gave the key to another one—he was different, of course.' Dani started to walk across the field. 'I did those self-defence classes. I got quite good.' Or she'd thought she had. Fortunately she hadn't had to test it out.

Alex was quiet. 'But you still get freaked in small spaces.'

'Silly, isn't it?' She laughed—still too high-pitched. 'Happened years ago. I should be over it by now. I mean, it was nothing. It wasn't that bad. What a wimp.'

'Don't.' He took her hand and stopped walking. 'Don't try to minimise it.'

Dani shut up at the touch of his fingers on hers, but it took a long time before she could bring herself to look at him.

'You must have been really scared.'

'I couldn't breathe,' Dani answered almost unconsciously.

'He was going to hurt you.' Alex's face hardened. 'He did hurt you.'

She shook her head. 'No. He didn't.'

'He did,' Alex said quietly. 'Maybe not as bad as he could have, as he wanted to, but he did hurt you.'

She had no answer to that.

'Your mum had lots of boyfriends.' Alex stated the obvious.

So? Dani's hackles rose and she pulled her hand away, instinctively wanting to karate chop him in the neck. Instead she took a second to breathe—and heard the way in which he'd spoken. He wasn't judging. He wasn't even asking. It was a plain statement of fact—nothing more. And so she nodded. 'And every time she thought she'd found the One.' Then she shook her head. 'There isn't a One. She was so naive—such a romantic fool. She let them walk all over her because she thought she loved them and she wanted them to love her. I won't be such a fool.'

'Not every guy wants to take advantage, Dani.'

'No?' She turned to face him. 'He was still taking advantage right up 'til the day she died.'

'Your dad?'

'Yeah.' Always he returned like a damn boomerang. How her mother could take him back time after time she never knew. He was—amongst other things—a convicted fraudster, how could she possibly believe a word he said? But Dani did know why—because she had wanted to believe him too. She'd wanted him to love her—he was her *father*.

Instead he used them both.

'You and your mum were close, huh?'

'For a lot of the time it was just the two of us.' Those were the best times. When her mother wasn't bending herself into any shape the new guy wanted—trying to please him, to keep him, to make him love her. She'd never seemed to feel able to just be herself. Because she was loveable. Her mother had been a fun, generous, wonderful woman. But she'd also been co-dependent, believing it was impossible to be happy if she didn't have a man.

'So you decided to have your joy boys rather than relationships? Is that what happened?'

She wrinkled her nose. She should never have made that lot up.

'How many were there, really?' He bent to look into her eyes, his own glinting.

'What is this? You going on *Mastermind* and your topic of choice is the scintillating life of Dani Russo?'

He chuckled. 'I'm betting one. Two at the most. *Boyfriends.*'

'You think you're so smart,' she grumbled. 'What is it you really want to know, Alex? You think one broke my heart? Put me off men?'

'Maybe,' he answered calmly. 'I want to know who and how.'

'I haven't been put off completely,' she said brazenly. 'I wouldn't be sleeping with you if I had.' She turned and started to run. 'Race you to the car!'

She had a good head start, but she knew he was fast. As she ran ahead of him the old memories flashed faster than her feet. Yes, she'd had a boyfriend. After almost making it through her teens without becoming a statistic as her mum had, she'd finally fallen for one of the neighbourhood guys—the older brother of another of her employer's cadets. He'd pursued her so hard and so sweetly—or so she'd believed. Only she'd been determinedly single for so long she hadn't known she'd become a sport to the gang of them—the ultimate challenge. It had taken him six months of occasional dates, but he'd won a crate of beer for being the one to bed her. He'd bragged and betrayed her intimate secrets.

She'd been such a naive idiot it was embarrassing and she didn't want to tell Alex a thing about that one. What was she doing going all Oprah-sofa-open anyway? He'd heard more than enough already.

He overtook her in the last five metres to the car—easily striding out, and she knew he'd been holding back to let her think she could win. She leant against the door, trying to catch her breath back. But it was impossible. She couldn't touch the bottom of this pool they were swimming in anymore. She was way out of her depth. She didn't want them to just be bed buddies. She didn't want this ever to end.

So she was just like every other woman who'd slept with him—once bitten, his forever. That was why all his old flames stayed friends with him—because their hope sprang eternal, that he'd go back to them. And she couldn't blame any of them. Because when he turned his full attentiveness on?

All-consuming delight.

She shivered. Was this the feeling that had made her mother act so stupidly time and time again? To get so stuck on someone that she became blind to all those glaringly obvious faults?

Except what were Alex's faults again?

Oh, that was right. He didn't want a *relationship*. He just liked sex. And she was merely his current playmate. But what about last night? It hadn't been a night of pure physical pleasure and release. It hadn't been that at all. It had been much more. There'd been no physical intimacy, but total emotional honesty. She'd opened up to him, cared for him—shown him. But hadn't he opened up to her too? She couldn't help hoping he had—because although he didn't know it, last night he'd got that last little pocket of her heart too.

'Let's go to the movies.' Alex hadn't been to the movies in years. It'd be like a date—following on from the afternoon in the park. He was still smiling about the sight of her running ahead of him and the basic instinct that had risen in him— driving him to overtake her. Really he'd just wanted to catch her close, for he was still feeling vicious about what had happened to her years before. He could hardly bear to think about it.

They went home to shower and change, then went to a pizza restaurant where she had one of her egg-and-spinach numbers. Then the movie.

If he'd hoped that taking her to a spooky thriller would have her pouncing into his lap halfway through, he'd have been disappointed. But as it was he'd have been disappointed if she *had*. No way was his wannabe street fighter going to be scared by some movie. No, it was the more subtle things that set her on edge. Like him calling her Danielle.

'It's such a pretty name.' He spread his hands peaceably when she glared at him across the table at the café after, her forkful of cake suspended mid-air.

'I prefer Dani.'

'Dani like a boy?'

Her chin tilted.

Yeah, that was it. As if an abbreviation of her pretty name could possibly desexualise her. She was the ultimate in feminine—soft and curvy, short and sweet—though she'd probably kill him if he said so. But he understood why she'd wanted to hide from the succession of men in her mother's life, why she made out as if she were Ms Aggressive Man Eater— she didn't trust people. And who could blame her? Hell, he knew how hard it was to trust—and Dani had every reason to be as wary as him. Like him she'd been betrayed by someone she should have been able to trust completely—a parent.

But if he'd decided to be some kind of a chivalrous gent, planning to take the time to woo her—to win her trust and then win her completely—he supposed he shouldn't take her to bed tonight. He should just kiss her softly good-night—hold her close and then gently break away. Bide his time and all that. But Alex hadn't conquered the finance markets by being slow. Alex won by seeing opportunities and seizing them.

And this was one advantage he knew he had and he was going to play it for all he was worth. Besides, he just couldn't help himself.

Once inside the door he turned her into his arms. But as he kissed her, a whole new depth of feeling arose. Really, he could kiss her for hours and instantly resolved to. He loved the promise of everything that he felt when he was with her—the feeling of such rightness. He didn't want to sleep with anyone else. But much more importantly than that, he wanted to see her happy. Hell, how he wanted that for her.

CHAPTER ELEVEN

DANI pushed back so she could look at Alex. Really look at him. He said nothing, but he met her gaze—unwaveringly, openly, devastatingly. She couldn't speak, couldn't move, could only stare at the warmth, the promise of absolutely everything in his eyes.

He moved to kiss her again, so slowly, with almost unbearable restraint. The gentleness seemed to flay her skin raw. Slow kisses, kisses that grew deeper and deeper still. Kisses that—she suddenly realised—were filled with infinite tenderness.

She started to shake.

His hands smoothed down her arms, settled on her waist and gently pulled her closer.

'We have all night,' he murmured, kissing her eyelids closed.

He made her feel as if they had forever.

Dani moved uncontrollably, absolutely undone by his slow sweetness. He kissed her, kept kissing her—raining them all over her face and neck and shoulders and breasts and returning, always returning to her mouth, for such intimate, deep caresses. She met him with the infinite, yearning need of her own. Her hands lifted. She too needed to touch, to caress, to *care*. She found him so beautiful.

They moved slowly, working their way upstairs. No words

interfered with the beautiful bliss of the moment—the magic between them too powerful to allow anything but truth in their actions.

Eventually, as inevitably as the sun set in the evening sky, their passion rose. Touches grew firmer, faster as their breathing roughened. The emotion that made her cling to him wasn't just born of a need deep in her belly, but from the core of her heart too: to be close—to be one.

And then they were. Their hands laced, bodies intertwined, breath mingling as she met his gaze in wonder. She heard his choked cry and felt the way he muttered her name. She never knew what she said in response—whether it was words or just the pure sound of an all emotional ecstasy that seemed to endlessly pour from her.

Long moments later he rolled, taking her with him so she sprawled over his broad chest, locking her in his arms so she was kept warm and snug and safe. Yet somehow she still felt as if she were flying. As if she'd been freed—able to soar higher and further than she'd ever dreamed was possible.

He drew the sheet up to cover them, his hand drawing gentle circles on her back, soothing her still-too-sensitive skin. Slowly her breathing regulated, matching the gentle rise and fall of his chest. Her muscles softened as she relaxed completely and his arms tightened just that little more. Utterly at peace, she slept.

Alex heard the beep of his phone. It was in his trousers, which had been shed halfway down the stairs. He thought about ignoring it. Except the workaholic in him couldn't. Carefully, he slipped out from beneath his sleeping sweetheart. The query took only a minute to deal with. From habit he flicked through the rest of the messages that had landed while he'd been so utterly lost in Dani. He paused as he saw the number. Quietly he went down into the study, locked the door and dialled. The investigator answered on the second ring.

'Tell me everything.'

Almost an hour later he put the phone down. Stared out of the window at the dark garden and tried to take it in. Tried to decide what the hell he was going to do about it. How on earth was he going to tell her?

He didn't want to. He just didn't want to.

He'd never thought of himself as a coward before, but right now he knew he was. Dani didn't want to be lonely anymore, did she? Sure, she said she didn't want relationships, didn't want a lover, but she wanted a family. That was why she wanted to find her brother. He shifted in his chair. Yeah. There it was. That flicker of jealousy. Her brother would have had more of a claim on her than Alex did. She wanted that kind of relationship, not any other. So stupid, so wrong of him to feel jealous of that. And why did he?

Because he wanted her himself. He wanted his own relationship with her.

But not like this. It didn't have to be one or the other. She should have had both. She should have had everything.

It was the one thing he knew would make her crumble. And he couldn't bear to be the one to destroy her hopes. She'd waited for so long, wanted for so long. But it wasn't to be. And he was going to have to tell her.

He really didn't want to.

And, yeah, there was that other selfish reason too, wasn't there—why he wasn't waking her, telling her right now as he should be?

He didn't want her to leave.

Once she knew, she'd walk out of his life. He knew it in

his bones. While she might be beginning to open up, it wasn't enough yet. He hadn't had enough time to build the kind of bridge he'd never before built, that he knew she hadn't built, and he was afraid of losing her.

So he wouldn't do it. Not yet. He'd wait for the morning. Besides—the lab tests hadn't come in. He could justify the delay then—sure he could. He'd wait until he had all the proof.

And then he'd tell her.

He walked back up the stairs, stared at the little lump she made in his bed. She stirred slightly as he slipped in beside her. He gently wrapped his arms around her, stroking her hair, soothing her back into sleep.

But the future pressed heavy on his heart. He wished like hell it had been different. It was too awful that he had Patrick wanting to mend fences with him, but that Dani was to have nothing—when she wanted and he didn't. She deserved so much more. He waited, watched as the sky lightened and wished he could make a bargain with either a god or a demon to trade her loss over to him. Hoped against hopelessness—prayed that in the darkness she would turn to him.

When she woke the sun was streaming in, and when she saw he was still there beside her, her colour mounted. She almost looked shy. 'Shouldn't you be up already answering a million messages or something?'

Alex managed a small smile. She wasn't happy with him staying in bed with her? His tough cookie felt uneasy when he spent so much time with her. Too bad, because he was about to spend a whole lot more. No matter what, he was determined to stick with her through this.

She was like a little wild cat. If you stretched out a hand to caress her you might get scratched. Even though inside she was yearning for that little bit of love, her first instinct was to defend. Because she couldn't be sure you weren't going to hurt her.

Alex figured he could handle a few surface scratches. It was worth it because when she did relax she was the softest, sweetest playmate—with that hint of snap-your-head-off danger. His whole point of focus had shifted. No longer was this about a spot of play in a time of stress. It was all about her.

Trust took time, though. And he didn't have a lot of time. He had to make quick progress—and he'd make the most of any advantage he had to do it.

He swallowed the guilt and reached for her—surely it would be worth it. He wanted her to have the day—not to know just yet. A few more hours until there was certainty. Then he'd tell her.

Dani couldn't put last night out of her head—the way they'd been together, the way he'd held her, so close and right through 'til the sun shone high and bright through the window. And the way he looked at her...

Oh, she was so under his spell, and dreaming of that ending common to all fairytales—the happy-ever-after one.

When she slid into his car after work he leaned over and kissed her—another of those kisses that combined the sweetest tenderness with the most sultry passion. She smiled at him, her heart in her throat, in her eyes, beating its message loud in her ears. Surely he must see and hear it and feel it too? He took her hand in his as he drove them home. She didn't think she'd ever felt so happy.

'It's a play premiere, right?' She checked on the plan as she changed.

He nodded.

She smoothed down her black dress. She was going to

have to go shopping soon—another outing in this number and she'd be letting Alex down.

His phone rang again.

'You better be sure to switch that off in the theatre.'

'Vibrate,' he muttered, looking at the screen and turning away to take the call.

Dani finished combing her hair and leant closer to the mirror to carefully slide in the hairclip and then do her lippy.

'Dani.'

She looked up to see his reflection, struck by the new note in his voice. The tux was gorgeous. But his face was ashen.

'Alex?' She spun to face him.

'I have to tell you something.'

Whatever it was, it wasn't going to be good. He looked worse than when he'd told her about Patrick. Only this wasn't about him, this was about her. She knew because of the way he was looking at her—as if he didn't want to.

'You've found him.'

'Yes.'

She almost couldn't bear to ask. He was looking so solemn. Why? What was wrong? What had happened? 'Why are you looking so serious?' She couldn't do anything more than whisper.

'Because it's not what you wanted, Dani.'

She couldn't breathe. 'He doesn't want to meet me?'

'No.' Alex pushed out a long breath. 'He's dead, Dani.'

'*What?*' She couldn't move. 'He's what?'

'His name was Jack Parker. He got adopted into a really nice family. Did fine at school. He was going into the family business—working with his father.'

'What happened?' She needed to know: how, when—dead? Had he really said *dead*?

'A car accident. It wasn't his fault—he was in the wrong place, at the wrong time.'

'He was killed.' She was staring, unblinking, but didn't know what she was seeing.

'He was in a coma for a couple of days and then he died. It was five years ago.'

Dani's heart just stopped. All of her stopped. *Five years ago?* He'd died before their mother. He'd died before Dani had even known about him.

'Dani?'

She forced herself to swallow. It seemed like a huge action, her whole body involved in the effort. She blinked. Alex was right in front of her, his hand outstretched as if he was about to take her arm. She turned away and forced in a long, controlled breath. 'That's great he found a family.'

'Yeah, they seem really nice,' Alex said quietly. 'They offered to meet with you, if you'd like. They have photos they'd share, would talk to you about him.'

Dani bent her head. 'I don't think that would be a good idea.'

'Dani—'

'I know now. That's all that matters. It's finished.'

'No, it isn't. It's only just started.'

Dani closed her eyes. No. She didn't want to think on this anymore. Not right now. She didn't want to take it in.

Jack Parker.

She pushed the name away—didn't want him to become real; it would only heighten the loss. What she needed now was oblivion. And she'd make the most of the opiate she had right here. She turned back to Alex, didn't look into his eyes, just looked at his broad chest. In her mind's eye she could see the muscles beneath the suit—he was the perfect instrument of pleasure. Even now she could see his whole body tense.

'Dani, you need—'

'Action.' She walked towards him.

'No, you need to talk. To me.'

'No.' She shook her head, and pressed against him. 'I need action. That's all.'

He caught her hands before she could even try to tease him into play. Damn. She could be mindless in less than a minute if only he'd touch her.

'This is too important. Dani. No.' His grip on her wrists eased, his thumbs stroking. 'It's OK to grieve, Dani.'

No, it wasn't. She didn't want to cry. She didn't want to feel anything—she just wanted to forget.

Because if she didn't forget it—and soon—she'd want to lean on Alex and cry. Dani never cried, certainly not in front of anyone. She drew on the iron will she'd built up inside her over the last year. She was not going to be weak—she was not going to let it out. She didn't want to be that vulnerable. Her heart hurt too much already. And if she acknowledged it, it would hurt more—she couldn't bear to be hurt more.

'There's nothing to grieve. I never even met him.' She denied it all. 'I wanted to know. Now I do.'

'No, you wanted family. You wanted someone.'

She shook her head. 'I don't need anyone.'

'Dani,' he admonished gently.

She stood still, fighting the gaping wound inside, determined to stop the hurt gushing out of her. She couldn't cope if it did. She couldn't let this become *real*. But she couldn't stop that last little thread of hope uncurling. 'You're sure. I mean, there's no doubt, is there? It's definitely him?'

'The DNA test proved it.'

'The DNA test?' Stunned, she pulled her wrists free and stared at him. 'What DNA test?'

There was no hiding the guilt in his face now.

'You did a DNA test without my knowing?' Her voice rose up into screech territory. 'How the hell did you do that—take a pubic hair or something?' She felt that violated.

'Dani.' He took her shoulders firmly.

'Did you dig up his grave?' Raw feeling surged through her veins—the kind of feeling that gave her the strength she needed right now—*anger*. 'How long have you known?' He had to have known something to get the tests done. 'Why didn't you tell me you thought you'd found him sooner?' Yes, it was easy to be angry. So easy to be furiously angry with Alex.

'I didn't want to get your hopes up until it was certain. I didn't want to hurt you.'

Well, right now she wanted to hurt him. 'So last night you knew.'

'I found out late last night. But I only got the lab confirmation in that call just now.'

She hardly heard him. So it had been pity that had driven his tenderness this morning. 'You're a bastard, Alex. You're such a bastard.'

'I know.'

'Oh, please.' She turned on him, striking out in her agony. 'You're still upset about your parentage? Come on, Alex, get over it.' She hurt so much and she wanted to hurt him more.

'Dani—' His fingers were painfully tight on her shoulders now and she was sure he was about to bodily chuck her out. And she'd be glad. She wanted everything to end.

But all he did was say softly, 'You're not taking it out on me.'

Alex badly wanted to take her in his arms, wanted to kiss her to stop the hurtful words. Like a trapped, wounded animal, she thought the only way to escape was to attack.

But he didn't draw her closer. Instead he stiffened his arms, holding her away so he could read her expression.

What he wanted was for her to lower her guard again and let him in. He ached to comfort her. She was so obviously devastated, but she was denying everything.

'You're right,' she said. 'Sorry.'

He watched, helpless, as she shut down—freezing him out completely. His fingers instinctively pressed harder into her bones—as if it were some way to bring her back to him—but she didn't even flinch. It was as if she were turning to marble before his eyes—a version of herself but with her beauty, her vitality, sucked out.

It crushed him. Already she was gone. And whatever closeness or intimacy he thought they'd been building over the last few days was revealed to be the sham it was. She trusted him no more than she had on day one. She was no less afraid.

Her brown eyes were almost black, like bottomless holes in a face too pale to be well. His heart contracted. 'Dani—'

'I'm going to…check my lipstick.' She twisted away and he let her go.

'You've just done your lipstick.' Her wretched lipstick was on the table. She was running away—not facing what he'd told her.

'We have this play to go to, don't we?' She picked up the lipstick and reapplied.

'No, I'll cancel—'

'There's no need to do that.' She carefully replaced the lid.

No. She wasn't one to crumble, was she? She denied all the way—refused to admit to weakness, hurt or need. But it would come out some time—it just had to. And he was damn sure he was going to be there when it did. He sighed. OK, maybe a little distraction might help. An hour or two in a theatre might give her a chance to think. No way would she concentrate on the play—her mind would wander.

And he was getting nowhere with her now and he didn't want her packing her bags in the next five minutes, which she'd probably do if they stayed at home. 'Are you sure you're up to it?'

'Of course I am.' She shoved her feet into her shoes.

Yeah, of course she was. Alex stuffed his fists into his pockets. 'Then let's go.'

It was a living hell. Ten minutes into it Alex was ready to leave. Dani was doing her zombie impression beside him. He covered her hand with his, hers was freezing. A trickle of dread slid down his spine and his eyes hurt from trying to read her expression in the dim light.

'Let's go,' he murmured in her ear as soon as the curtain went down on the first act.

Deathly pale now, she swayed as she stood. Was the shock wearing off and the reality hitting her? He wished she'd talk to him. He needed to get her home so he could make her talk to him.

'I'm just going to freshen up.'

In other words go put on her armour. She'd run away for a few minutes and try to pull herself together. Except she was so on edge he didn't think it was going to work this time. The sooner he got her home, the better. He'd hold her close, just hold her in his arms and cradle her until those tears came. She needed it. Hell, *he* needed it.

Dani blindly followed Alex to the car. Trying really hard not to think. But her brain was screaming—she had to run, she had to hide from this truth. 'I'm going back to Australia,' she said as he drove home.

'Not yet, Dani. You've had a shock—you need time to take it in.' His eyes were dark.

'I want to move out.'

'You don't want to talk?' He looked at her searchingly. 'Don't you think we both could do with a little comfort right now? Some companionship? At the very least, aren't we friends?'

His words thickened the ice around her heart. He'd said they couldn't be friends. And they couldn't. He was much more than that to her. 'You have other friends. You have Lorenzo.'

'I haven't told him about my father. I haven't told anyone but you.'

A tiny bird fluttered its wings, wanting to fly in her heart. Silly to be so moved by that one little comment and its implication of intimacy, of trust. Surely she couldn't trust it—it was just that she'd been there at the time when he'd needed to share. She couldn't believe it was anything more than that. She couldn't believe in anything right now. 'I really want to go, Alex.'

'Not tonight.'

Dully, she supposed he was right. Where would she go? It wasn't practical. He was so generous, wasn't he? But she didn't want any more of his tender pity. 'OK, but I need to be alone.'

He swallowed. 'Sure.'

'I promised Sara I'd go to the meeting on Monday. I said I'd be there when she delivered her presentation. I'll go after that.' It was all she could think. She couldn't let her down.

She'd let her mother down.

When they reached the house, she took far too much care undoing her seat belt but he didn't even move. When she looked at him he was staring at the garage wall, his face so expressionless she wondered if he'd even heard her. She slipped out of the car and suddenly picked up speed. She'd meant it. She needed tonight to be alone to lock away her demons.

But he moved faster, grabbing her hand as she got to the lounge. She stopped. Eyes closed, she kept her back to him. 'Don't—'

His fingers squeezed hard.

'You know where I am if you need me.' His voice was so husky it shattered her. She swayed, holding on by the last thread.

But he let her hand go and walked past her, going straight up the stairs, not looking back.

She stared at nothing as he disappeared, utterly unable to move. She couldn't let herself need him.

Hours later she stumbled to the kitchen, poured a glass of iced water and didn't look at the tray on the table she knew was meant for her.

'You're staying home today.' He walked up to her and touched her nose with a light finger. 'You're tired.'

So was he, but he was in his suit and ready to go. She was no less capable than him. 'I can go.'

'Stay home, Dani. You need to.' He was gone before she could reply.

She sipped the icy water and glanced at the plates he'd prepared for her—fruit salad, a bagel, juice. Then she saw the file on the other side. She didn't need to open it to know what it was—the information from the private investigator. Alex had left it deliberately for sure. She stared at it as if it were more terrifying than an armed intruder.

Jack Parker.

Could she bear to know any more than that?

She perched on the edge of one of the dining chairs. Pulled the folder towards her. She turned the cover, read the words. Dates, school—it was like a CV. How could someone's life be reduced to a couple of A4 pages?

She turned the next page and stopped.

Photos. A baby, a boy, a youth. Brown eyes. Brown hair. Like hers. So much like hers.

She slammed the file shut. Pain burning her inside out. She couldn't do it. Couldn't bear to see what she'd lost before she'd even been able to find it. Couldn't bear to face the fact that she'd failed her mother.

She stood. Ran. She wasn't going to sit here and mope all day. There was work to be done at the Whistle Fund. She wasn't going to let Cara down.

Cara looked up when she walked in, a surprised smile brightening her face. 'I didn't expect to see you today. Alex called to say you weren't feeling well.'

'Just a slight headache,' Dani covered. 'Gosh, if you can work with morning sickness then I can manage a mild headache.'

Cara laughed. 'I haven't had a single bout of morning sickness. Been eating like a horse from the moment I got pregnant.'

Dani sat sharply. 'You haven't been sick at all?'

She watched Cara shake her head. Saw how her eyes sparkled, and her skin glowed. This was a woman for whom pregnancy was a piece of cake. Painful realisation dawned. 'You don't really need me here, do you?'

'Well…' Cara blushed '…there's always too much work to do. I mean, usually we get other volunteers, but now we have you…'

Dani rubbed her head and felt the icy sweat beading on her brow. 'Do you do this voluntarily?'

'They insist on paying me something, but I give it back to them by buying lots of tickets to whatever they've got going. I, um…' she was blushing even harder '…I don't really need to work.' She said it as if it were something to be ashamed of.

Dani forced a smile to reassure her. But inside she was trying to process the info that should have been blindingly obvious before now. How could she not have worked this out already? Cara was a nominally paid volunteer, working part-time hours. Whereas she was getting paid top temp dollar—full-time.

But it wasn't the charity paying her wages at all. It was Alex. And *she* was the charity. She cringed. The whole thing was a charade. He'd felt bad about what had happened, and this was him taking care of it. He'd said duty to the Carlisle business had been instilled in him from birth. But his sense of duty extended in all areas of his life too. And when he'd played a part in her life being stuffed up, he'd taken every step to help. Duty—not desire.

And now pity.

While he might have wanted to play with her for a bit, she bet he hadn't meant for it to turn into this almighty mess. For she wasn't Alex Carlisle standard—she wasn't like those princesses at the charity—like Cara. She couldn't even begin to compare.

'Cara, I'm really sorry, but my head actually is a bit bad.' Dani stood.

'Oh, do you want me to—?'

'I'll be fine. I'll just go home again.'

Except there was no home, was there?

She raced to her room as soon as she got back into his house. It only took moments to throw her belongings into her pack. But she'd barely started tugging on the zip when she heard the garage door.

He was up the stairs with Superman speed.

'Lorenzo called.' He walked into the middle of her room. 'Cara said you'd come to work and then gone again almost immediately. She was worried.' He looked at her bag. When he spoke again, his voice was colder than ice. 'Were you going to leave a note?'

'Yes.'

'Written it yet?'

'No.'

'So tell me.'

'There's no need for me to stay anymore. I've found out all I needed to.'

'What about Sara and the meeting?'

'She doesn't need me. She probably won't even notice I'm not there. And *Cara* doesn't need me, does she?' she said bitterly.

His mouth tightened. 'What about me?'

'You don't need me, either.' And in another week he'd have someone else in her place.

'What if I told you I did?' He stepped closer. 'What if I told you I wanted you to stay? Would you?'

She shook her head. Not trusting her voice. For how long would he want her—how long 'til they became 'just friends'. She couldn't do that.

'What if I said we have something special?'

'What we have is good sex. That's all.'

'So you're just going to run away? From me? From this?' He threw Jack's file at her.

She turned away as the pages scattered on the floor. 'I don't want it.' Her voice broke. 'I don't want…'

'Don't want what?'

She turned back. 'To stay.'

He walked right into her space. 'I won't let you go.'

'You can't stop me.' She pushed past him and picked up her bag.

'You think you're so tough. But you're not. You're scared. You're that total chicken.'

So what if he was right? So what if she was dying inside? She wasn't going to hurt herself more by lingering in an affair that had no future. She couldn't handle any more of the agony burning her through now. 'I told you from the start I don't do relationships.'

'What the hell do you think we've been doing? We've been living together, being together, *making love* together—that's not a relationship?'

'We didn't make love. We had no-strings, uncomplicated sex!' How could he say otherwise? It was him feeling bad for her—his caretaker duty on full steam ahead—but she wasn't his new pity project. 'We were flatmates trading favours—nothing more than that. Not a relationship.'

'That's ridiculous. What is it going to take, Dani?' He gripped her arm. 'When are you going to face up to your fears? When are you going to let yourself trust someone? When are you going to let someone in? Because until you do, you're going to be alone and lonely.'

'Alone is exactly what I want to be.' Alone meant there'd be no more loss. No more crippling heartache. She yanked her arm free and raced down the stairs.

'I want you to stay.' He kept pace. 'I want you.'

She ran to the front door.

'Did you hear what I said, Dani? I want you.'

Yeah, but the want wouldn't last—the want would die. Everything else had been based on him feeling responsible, feeling guilty, feeling pity. None of which would last, either. So she turned, faced him down. 'Well, I don't want you.'

'Liar. You want me just as much as I want you. You can't say no to me.'

'No!' she shouted. 'I'm saying it now. I don't want you.'

And it wasn't all a lie. For she didn't. She didn't want him like this.

CHAPTER TWELVE

'You have to get out of this office, Alex.'

'You'll just have to manage alone tonight, Renz. I'm sure you can handle it.'

Lorenzo had his hands on his hips. 'It'll be a good night.'

'Are we going to settle this the old way?' A hard out physical battle might just be the thing. At least it might wear him out enough to crash.

'I couldn't do it to you,' Lorenzo grumbled. 'The way you look, I'd knock you out first punch. Haven't you been sleeping at all?'

Three days. Three long, lonely, bloody miserable days that had dra-a-aged. No, he hadn't slept at all. In his head that row played over and over and over—preventing any kind of wind-down of body or mind.

Could he have been more lovelorn teen? Throwing the most desperate lines at her—'I won't let you go'—what, like he was going to imprison her?

He wished he could have.

Damn, it still hurt.

She wouldn't give them a chance. She wouldn't let him in.

'Have you heard from her?'

'No.'

'Do you know where she is?'

'Yes.' He'd had someone track her from the moment she'd left—as awful as that was. He'd never used a private investigator in his life before, but in the last month he'd spent more on one than a footballer's wife spent on botox for a year. 'But that's not the point.' He wanted her to come back. He wanted *her* to want to. But it looked as if that wasn't going to happen.

Lorenzo stared at him, his eyes darker than the moonless night. 'You're not going after her?'

'No.'

Alex sat in the silence after Lorenzo had gone. Eventually acknowledged to himself that he'd lied to his friend. Another lie—this time to try to stop himself from hurting. It hadn't worked. He could wait another day, maybe two, but then he had to go after her. He didn't know what he was going to do when he got to her, but somehow he would win. He checked his phone again, saw the little icon flashing. There'd been many messages now, and he'd ignored every one. But he couldn't ignore it anymore—had to have closure on something at least.

'Alex?' Patrick answered right away, sounded surprised.

'Yeah, ah, sorry I haven't got back to you sooner.' Alex grimaced, what was *he* doing apologising? A spurt of irritation heated him, driving his words. 'Look, I had a great father. He was fantastic. I don't need another.'

Samuel had been there for him, had loved him. He truly was his dad and Alex wasn't going to let anyone take that from either of them.

There was a pause. Patrick cleared his throat. 'I understand.'

Elbow on his desk, Alex shut his eyes and massaged round them with thumb and middle finger. Was that edge of disappointment genuine?

Yeah, he thought it was—it resonated with the disappointment deep in his own bones. 'But maybe, um…' his voice failed '…maybe I could do with a friend.'

He didn't really know if it was going to be possible. It was a huge chasm between them, a pit of bad history miles wide. But he'd learned from Dani: things were never black-and-white and, hell, it was so hard to tell someone you loved something that was going to hurt them. Every instinct was to protect, as his mother had wanted to protect both him and Samuel—he could acknowledge that now. It didn't make it right, but he understood why people sometimes lied. And he so badly wanted to be given another chance, surely he could offer one himself.

'That would be great, Alex,' Patrick said quietly. 'Thanks.'

'I thought you'd have been on a plane back to Oz days ago.'

Dani looked up from where she was staring at the bowl of sugar sachets in the café down by the waterfront. Lorenzo. Looking as unreadable as ever. Although his vibe was definitely one of disapproval.

'I am. Tomorrow.' She was working up to it. But there'd been one last thing she'd had to do first. Now even that was done.

'Then you need to go and see him today.'

Dani shook her head. 'He was doing me a favour because he felt bad about the video thing. He felt responsible. That's all it was.' He was doing what he thought he should. His sense of duty had driven him. And with all the stress he was under, things had got confused. But she was as right for him as an electric blanket was right for a snowman. She'd wanted to get out before he woke up to that fact. She just couldn't handle the heartache.

'Look, I've known Alex a long time and I've never known him to do something he doesn't want to. He's a smart guy—

he knows what he's doing,' Lorenzo said. 'I've never known him to move a woman in with him. He could have put you up in a hotel. He could have given you some money and walked away.'

'He's too meticulous to have done that. He wanted to be sure I was OK.'

'No. The Alex I know would never have taken a woman to his home in that situation for fear she'd get the wrong impression. He's always been very careful not to lead anyone on.'

Yeah, she knew that—for him it was 'just sex, just fun'.

'But it seems you've got the totally wrong impression anyway.' Lorenzo pulled out the chair beside her and sat. 'I don't like to see my friend hurting. Seems to me you're not that happy, either.'

Dani shook her head. For her it hadn't been just sex. It had been everything. Deep inside her that flicker of hope had refused to be snuffed. Lorenzo's words made it burn brighter than the sun. It took her three minutes to summon up courage to ask him. 'Do you think he meant it?'

'I think you need to ask him that yourself.'

Her heart thudded, more adrenalin flooding her than that time she'd been too scared to even blink. Could she ask him?

It was then that she realised just how brave her mother had been—to take the chance, to want to believe, every time. Even if it meant her heart might get squished. She'd always tried; she'd always taken the risk.

Dani had fought so long to be strong. To be independent. But now she saw she hadn't been at all. She was exactly what Alex had said—a coward. Had he been right about other things too?

She thought about Jack—his life had ended way before it should have. Her mother had died too young too. So she had to take the chance—she had to do it for them—she had to be brave and take life's risks on.

Dani turned to Lorenzo. 'Can I ask a favour?'

Alex worked late again. Left a message for his housekeeper to leave his dinner in the fridge; he'd microwave it later. The little he could be bothered eating tasted no good anyway. After nine, he walked out onto the balcony off his office, not caring about how cold and dark it was out there. Just needed the chill wind to whistle into his ears and blank out the angry voice yelling at him. His angry voice—berating himself for screwing it up so royally. And then the smaller voice wondered how on earth he was going to fix it. Nothing could stop the thoughts. Nothing numbed the pain from the knives twisting inside.

Eventually the freezing air bit hard enough to send him back indoors. He walked faster when he heard his mobile ringing. He picked it up just before it went to the answering machine. 'What?'

'Where the hell have you been?' Lorenzo bellowed.

Alex's brows rose and he held the phone a little from his ear. 'For a walk.'

'Without your *phone*?' Lorenzo never sounded emotional and here he was practically screeching at him.

Alex iced up inside, as well as out. 'What is it?'

'She called me. Wanted to set it up. But she's been there for ages.'

'Been where?' Damn it, couldn't Lorenzo make sense?

'Look at your computer—I sent you the link. You're supposed to be slaving at your desk, not getting fresh flipping air.'

Alex clicked the link and watched as the live webcast came on. No way.

'You'd better get moving, Alex. She's been waiting fifteen minutes already. She probably thinks you aren't coming.'

Alex swore. 'Why the hell is she in the lift?'

'It was her idea.'

Alex chucked the phone and ran.

Whichever daytime TV shrink it was who said confronting your fears was the way to free yourself needed to see a shrink themselves, because Dani was so not getting over her fears right now. Not any of them. In fact, they were worsening with every passing second. She had visions of herself riding up and down in the elevator for days—slowly starving, leaving only a skeleton for the security men to discover in ten months' time. Never mind the reality that only tomorrow people would arrive for work and find her there—a complete saddo but still alive. No, right now she'd rather indulge in the total drama girl-lost-in-lift-for-ever nightmare.

And when Alex found out he'd wince, hadn't realised he'd hurt her so much—he hadn't meant to, of course…thought she'd understood it was just an *arrangement*. Bed buddies and all that.

Because he hadn't meant it. He didn't want her.

If he did, he'd be here already.

She wiped her eye quickly, outraged that the tear had actually escaped her brimming rims. She never cried. Never, never, never.

Only now there was another tear. And another, and they wouldn't stop.

She turned her back to the damn camera and fished in her pocket. Double damn. No hanky, no tissue. Never necessary because she never cried. So she had to swish them away with her fingers again and sniff.

Ugh.

Now her fingers had black smudges on them because the mascara she'd applied with such excited care was running everywhere.

Great.

The lift wasn't even going up and down anymore. She couldn't be bothered getting up to press the buttons. Instead she just scrunched down, her back against the wall, her feet tucked underneath her. Lorenzo would probably take pity on her some time soon and come and tell her to give up and get out.

Yeah, it had happened. The lift was going up again. She buried her face in her hands, not wanting to see him. Beyond humiliated, beyond scared, she breathed short and fast, trying to hold back the wail that wanted release. If only she could ease the pain.

Large hands grasped her wrists and pulled hard, hauling her out of the lift.

'Can you breathe? Can you breathe, Dani?'

Alex. Oh, God, it was Alex. She could hardly see him through the tears streaming, but she felt his heat, his strength. She heard him.

'You're crying.' He sounded shocked. 'It's OK, honey, you're not in there anymore. You're out of there.' His hands rubbed over her back, pulling her hard against his strong frame. Oh, he was so warm. 'You're safe, Dani. You're safe.'

She hiccupped. He thought she was upset because she'd been in the lift? 'That's…that's not why I'm crying.'

His hands slowed on her back, relaxing the pressure, and she was able to pull away enough to tilt her head and look him in the eyes. 'I thought you weren't coming.'

For a moment she watched as he froze completely—his gaze boring into her. Then she couldn't bear it anymore and buried her face back in his chest. Too bad if he cared—his shirt was getting a soaking. But his arms clamped around her again—this time so hard she almost couldn't breathe.

'You lied to me.' He spoke softly, not relaxing his hold even a fraction.

'You lied to me too.' She closed her eyes but the tears still slipped beneath her lids. 'I guess the question is why did we lie?'

He slid his hand up her back, threading his fingers into the hair at the nape of her neck, angling her head so she felt his breath skim over her skin.

'I didn't tell you about finding out about your brother sooner for two reasons,' he said, his mouth millimetres from her ear. 'One, because I didn't want to hurt you—I knew you'd be upset. And two, I didn't want us to be over. I thought you'd leave as soon as you found out. I've been such an idiot, Dani. I thought we were just a fling. But we're not. We're forever. And I couldn't get that through to you before you left.'

He moved even closer, the warmth of his body melting hers so she leaned into him. His lips brushed her skin now— making her feel every word, as well as hear them.

'I know you don't believe in romance. You don't believe in love at first sight. But I sure as hell believe in lust at first sight. That's how it was between us. The chemistry just flared. You know that. I thought I was acting crazy because I'd found out about Patrick and needing you was a weird kind of release. But the fact is I'm just not in control about how I feel about you. Haven't been from the moment I laid eyes on you. And the more I got to know you, the more I felt for you, the more I wanted you. Barbs and all.'

'What do you mean, barbs?' She sniffed.

'I mean, the cold war concrete-wall, razor-wire, rooftop-sniper defence system you've got going.' His chest moved as he chuckled. 'But it's not going to work, Dani. Want to know why?'

She moved her head—a shake or a nod, not even she knew which it was.

'Because I love you. And I'm thinking maybe you love me too.'

'You think?' Her voice wobbled.

'You're here,' he said huskily. 'You've come back to me.'

She had. She nodded for certain then, her fingers curling into his arms, unashamedly clinging to him.

'When I'm with you, I'm happier than I have ever been,' Alex muttered. 'You light up my world. It's that simple.'

For a long moment Dani couldn't speak. But when she started she found it was easy. 'I lied to you because I was scared. I told you I didn't want you because I was scared about the strength of my feelings for you. And I was scared you didn't feel the same.' She took a shaky breath. 'I didn't want you thinking you were stuck with me. I didn't want to be the charity case that trapped you. I didn't want you to be with me out of pity.'

'Dani,' he groaned. 'I care about you. I want to take care of you. That's what people who love each other do. That's love, that's family. That's going to be our family. We've both been alone too long, Dani. You said you don't believe in relationships, but why were you looking for your brother? What did you hope to find when you found him if not some kind of a relationship? If not some family to love and be loved by?'

Tears flooded her eyes again. 'And I wanted to tell him how sorry she was. I promised her I would.'

'Oh, Dani.' He framed her face with gentle palms. 'Maybe she's found him now, huh? Maybe she's been able to tell him herself.'

'I hope so.' She breathed in courage. 'But you're right, Alex. I wanted to find him for me too. I don't know what I hoped for, really. But I was lonely. I wanted to find someone safe.'

'I'm the safest bet there is, Dani. Don't you know? I've the best credit rating you can get.' He smiled, joking just a little. 'Safer than any other finance company. Or any other man. Loving someone, wanting to care, isn't a weakness. Opening up takes strength. And you're the strongest person I've ever met.'

'I'm not. You were right before. I'm a coward,' she whispered. 'But I don't want to be anymore.' She drew in a shaky breath. 'I went to Jack's grave.'

'Dani.' He locked her in a bear hug. 'Alone?'

The tears streamed down her face as he cradled her.

'It's OK. It's OK.' She tried to say it so she'd believe it, but he shushed her. And at that she let all that was in her heart out—her sorrow, loneliness, and her love. Crying until the tears finally ran dry. And he just waited, just held her.

Neither of them alone now.

Long minutes later he brushed her silly fringe back behind her ear. 'I can't believe you were waiting in the lift.'

'I wanted to prove I could face my fears.'

'Tell you what, when we get home I'll shut us both in a cupboard and show you such a good time you'll never be afraid of small spaces again, OK?'

Oh, how that smile melted her. 'It might take more than one therapy session to cure me of the phobia.'

'Maybe.' He nodded solemnly. 'But we can only try, right? We face the fears together. Dani, you're determined, you're self-reliant, you're independent. I love how you fight your corner. But your corner is my corner too. From here on in we're on the same team, darling. We're building a life together.'

'Oh.' She swept her hand down his chest, totally floored by his flattery and feeling the need for some light, sarcastic relief. 'So it wasn't my boobs that caught your eye?'

He laughed, a wicked look lighting up his face. 'OK, so

they were the first thing I noticed. You guessed that already. But I took in the rest of you too—you're beautiful. I love the whole package that is you.'

She really was Carlisle standard? She was crazy pleased and her confidence blossomed. 'It's OK.' She moved sassily. 'You can like my boobs. I like your butt.'

'Oh, you do?'

'And your shoulders. And you have fantastic hands.'

'Yeah?'

'They're big enough to hold me.' She took his hand and placed it beneath her breast. He immediately spread his fingers, pushing up a little to take her weight, his thumb seeking her taut peak. Oh, that was what she wanted. 'There isn't a security camera in here, is there?'

'No.' His eyes dropped to her chest.

'The security guard isn't about to do his rounds?'

'He should be on the desk downstairs. I'll lock the door in case.' Alex backed her up against it. 'He knows I've been working late this week.'

She watched him watch her body respond to the simple, slow movement of his fingers. His eyes were hooded, pupils huge. His breathing more audible, but she was panting already. 'Please,' she whispered.

His gaze flicked up to hers. 'Please what?'

'Love me.'

His smile made her whole body heat with desire so sweet she almost couldn't bear it. And she believed it. Finally she truly believed it. 'Oh, Alex.' Overcome, she sobbed.

He kissed her. 'I do love you.'

His mouth was pure heaven. Filling her with pleasure and heat and she kissed him back with all her heart. Nothing held back. She pressed against him, needing to show him, to make him understand all that he meant to her. She threw her arms around his neck—loving him.

He was shaking, his hands moving fast. Somehow they did it, somehow not breaking that most sacred, searing kiss they moved enough to touch where they needed to touch, to become one, to feel the ecstasy that they could feel only with each other.

'I love you,' she breathed. 'I love this.'

Her legs wrapped around him as they had that day in the lift, her body rapturously absorbed his and the power surged between them. Like a flash of lightning it hit—so fast—her body shuddering as he cried out.

Afterwards he growled, practically flattening her against the door, his breathing rapid, his sweat dripping. 'How does it keep getting better?'

It was her turn to smile—that loving smile of total certainty.

He pushed away from her enough to gaze at her, ran his finger down her jaw and pushed that hair behind her ear again. 'You know, I have something for you.' A brief tease of a kiss before he pulled his trousers up and put his hand in his pocket. 'I've been carrying it forever, waiting to be able to give it to you.'

The solitaire was tear-shaped; it gleamed rather than sparkled—as if it was full of the sweetest promise. But what she loved even more was the setting, the thin gold and the pretty engraving on the band. It was unusual. And quite, quite girly. And inside she loved girly. So pretty. Just the thing she would have chosen for herself—not that she'd ever contemplated diamond engagement rings before. He held the ring on an angle so she could see the words etched on the inside.

Alex loves Dani.

Her silly eyes were watering again. But she went bold. 'It might get lonely being the only ring on that finger.'

'Oh, I already have a mate for it. A very pretty band. And I have a date for when I'm going to give it to you.'

'A date?'

'In just a couple of weeks, actually.'

'Alex,' she teased. 'Have you been organising?'

'Sure have. Everything.' He caught her hand. 'You can't muck up my plans now. I've got it all perfectly under control.'

'You've always got the answers, haven't you? Just the way you like it.' She watched as the ring slid down.

'Yeah, but it's been hell waiting for you, Dani.'

'I'm sorry.' She was. Her emotions still so raw she felt terrible for doing that.

He laughed then and pulled her close. 'It's OK. You have the rest of your life to make it up to me.'

'Yes.' She snuggled into his embrace and felt the magic between them healing her. 'I do.'

HARLEQUIN® *Presents*

Coming Next Month

from **Harlequin Presents®**. Available December 28, 2010.

#2963 THE RELUCTANT SURRENDER
Penny Jordan
The Parenti Dynasty

#2964 ANNIE AND THE RED-HOT ITALIAN
Carole Mortimer
The Balfour Brides

#2965 THE BRIDE THIEF
Jennie Lucas

#2966 THE LAST KOLOVSKY PLAYBOY
Carol Marinelli

#2967 THE SOCITY WIFE
India Grey
Bride on Approval

#2968 RECKLESS IN PARADISE
Trish Morey

Coming Next Month

from **Harlequin Presents®** EXTRA. Available January 11, 2011.

#133 THE MAN BEHIND THE MASK
Maggie Cox
From Rags to Riches

#134 MASTER OF BELLA TERRA
Christina Hollis
From Rags to Riches

#135 CHAMPAGNE WITH A CELEBRITY
Kate Hardy
One Night at a Wedding

#136 FRONT PAGE AFFAIR
Mira Lyn Kelly
One Night at a Wedding

REQUEST YOUR
FREE BOOKS!

HARLEQUIN® *Presents* ®

2 FREE NOVELS PLUS
2 FREE GIFTS!

PASSION GUARANTEED SEDUCTION

YES! Please send me 2 FREE Harlequin Presents® novels and my 2 FREE gifts (gifts are worth about $10). After receiving them, if I don't wish to receive any more books, I can return the shipping statement marked "cancel." If I don't cancel, I will receive 6 brand-new novels every month and be billed just $4.05 per book in the U.S. or $4.74 per book in Canada. That's a saving of at least 15% off the cover price! It's quite a bargain! Shipping and handling is just 50¢ per book.* I understand that accepting the 2 free books and gifts places me under no obligation to buy anything. I can always return a shipment and cancel at any time. Even if I never buy another book, the two free books and gifts are mine to keep forever.

106/306 HDN E5M4

Name _____ (PLEASE PRINT) _____

Address _____ Apt. # _____

City _____ State/Prov. _____ Zip/Postal Code _____

Signature (if under 18, a parent or guardian must sign)

Mail to the Harlequin Reader Service:
IN U.S.A.: P.O. Box 1867, Buffalo, NY 14240-1867
IN CANADA: P.O. Box 609, Fort Erie, Ontario L2A 5X3

Not valid for current subscribers to Harlequin Presents books.

Are you a current subscriber to Harlequin Presents books and want to receive the larger-print edition? Call 1-800-873-8635 today!

* Terms and prices subject to change without notice. Prices do not include applicable taxes. N.Y. residents add applicable sales tax. Canadian residents will be charged applicable provincial taxes and GST. Offer not valid in Quebec. This offer is limited to one order per household. All orders subject to approval. Credit or debit balances in a customer's account(s) may be offset by any other outstanding balance owed by or to the customer. Please allow 4 to 6 weeks for delivery. Offer available while quantities last.

Your Privacy: Harlequin Books is committed to protecting your privacy. Our Privacy Policy is available online at www.eHarlequin.com or upon request from the Reader Service. From time to time we make our lists of customers available to reputable third parties who may have a product or service of interest to you. If you would prefer we not share your name and address, please check here. ☐

Help us get it right—We strive for accurate, respectful and relevant communications. To clarify or modify your communication preferences, visit us at www.ReaderService.com/consumerchoice.

HP10R

HARLEQUIN®

A *Romance*

FOR EVERY MOOD™

Spotlight on
Classic

Quintessential, modern love stories
that are romance at its finest.

See the next page
to enjoy a sneak peek from
the Harlequin Presents® series.

*Harlequin Presents® is thrilled
to introduce the first installment of
an epic tale of passion and drama by*
**USA TODAY Bestselling Author
Penny Jordan!**

*When buttoned-up Giselle first meets
the devastatingly handsome Saul Parenti,
the heat between them is explosive....*

"LET ME GET THIS STRAIGHT. Are you actually suggesting that I would stoop to that kind of game playing?"

Saul came out from behind his desk and walked toward her. Giselle could smell his hot male scent and it was making her dizzy, igniting a low, dull, pulsing ache that was taking over her whole body.

Giselle defended her suspicions. "You don't want me here."

"No," Saul agreed, "I don't."

And then he did what he had sworn he would not do, cursing himself beneath his breath as he reached for her, pulling her fiercely into his arms and kissing her with all the pent-up fury she had aroused in him from the moment he had first seen her.

Giselle certainly *wanted* to resist him. But the hand she raised to push him away developed a will of its own and was sliding along his bare arm beneath the sleeve of his shirt, and the body that should have been arching away from him was instead melting into him.

Beneath the pressure of his kiss he could feel and taste her gasp of undeniable response to him. He wanted to devour her, take her and drive them both until they were equally satiated—even whilst the anger within him that she should make him feel that way roared and burned its resentment of his need.

She was helpless, Giselle recognized, totally unable to withstand the storm lashing at her, able only to cling to the man who was the cause of it and pray that she would survive.

Somewhere else in the building a door banged. The sound exploded into the sensual tension that had enclosed them, driving them apart. Saul's chest was rising and falling as he fought for control; Giselle's whole body was trembling.

Without a word she turned and ran.

Find out what happens when Saul and Giselle succumb to their irresistible desire in

THE RELUCTANT SURRENDER

Available January 2011 from Harlequin Presents®

MARGARET WAY

Wealthy Australian,
Secret Son

Rohan was Charlotte's shining white knight
until he disappeared—before she had
the chance to tell him she was pregnant.

But when Rohan returns years later as
a self-made millionaire, could the blond,
blue-eyed little boy and Charlotte's heart
keep him from leaving again?

Available January 2011

www.eHarlequin.com

HR17704